RETURN
to
MOROCCO

Norma Johnston

FOUR WINDS PRESS

New York

Four Winds Press
Macmillan Publishing Company
866 Third Avenue, New York, NY 10022
Collier Macmillan Canada, Inc.
First Edition
Printed in the United States of America

10 9 8 7 6 5 4 3 2 1

The text of this book is set in 12 point Simoncini Garamond.

Library of Congress Cataloging-in-Publication Data

Johnston, Norma.
Return to Morocco / by Norma Johnston. — 1st ed.   p.   cm.
Summary: Shortly after she and her grandmother arrive in Morocco,
seventeen-year-old Tori finds herself faced with sudden death and a
secret from her grandmother's past.
ISBN 0-02-747712-6
[1. Grandmothers—Fiction.   2. Morocco—Fiction.   3. Spies—Fiction.
4. Mystery and detective stories.]   I. Title.
PZ7.J6453Re 1988   [Fic]—dc19
88-6880   CIP   AC

For Dale Catherine

1   Where I come from, which is Texas, there are things you're expected to do. It doesn't matter whether you *like* the things or not. When your mother or your father introduces you to them, you better say "yes, ma'am" or "yes, sir" and start doing.

For instance, if your mother's involved, like mine is, with some charity that holds fund-raising debutante balls, you make your debut. But there's one thing I loathe: being manipulated. Or conned. I knew perfectly well the real reason Mother wanted me to make my debut: to teach me charm and poise. To help me to learn how to make inoffensive small talk instead of saying what's on my mind, and to smile a lot, no matter how I really feel. In other words, to learn how to become the perfect executive wife, like Mama. No, thanks!

That's what I made the mistake of saying during our big mother-daughter fight at the end of May.

"What do you *mean*, you're not going to make your debut?" Mama cried, aghast. "Don't you realize how this is going to look? It's Good Samaritan Hospital's biggest fund-raiser of the year! I'm the chairman of the ball committee, and your daddy's on the hospital board!"

Unfortunately, I did realize all that. But it didn't help. I was trapped between embarrassing my parents and being unable to live with myself, and I really did think that was too much to ask.

Don't get me wrong. I do love my parents. I even like them. It's just that Mama believes in diplomacy and conciliation and little white lies to make other people feel better (not that I was allowed to tell her any). I believe in the truth, the whole truth, and nothing but the truth. Which means we've been on a collision course since my fifth birthday party, when I said what I thought Granddaddy's cigar smoke smelled like.

My problem is that I tend to blurt out exactly what I'm thinking. That's why I wasn't getting anywhere in explaining why I couldn't go through all that stupid role-playing, pretending to be "introduced to society" when here I was seventeen and had known all the people I'd be presented to all my life. And I was dumb enough to tell Mama that I also couldn't face pretending to be a charming Southern Belle when I'd just broken up with Buck, the guy I'd been dating all through my sophomore and junior years.

He was captain of the football team, and a really easygoing, sweet-tempered guy, even though I guess I'd started to take him for granted. He'd been grabbed by Sue Hopper, who'd been after him since seventh grade. I didn't trust myself to be around the two of them at the ball.

I'd just finished explaining all that, when Mama started loading on the guilt about Good Samaritan. Then something in me snapped. I shouted out that Mama cared more about public appearances than about the hospital, which was mean of me and also totally unjust. But I didn't care at the time. I ran to the telephone and spilled my guts to Nannie.

Nannie is Nancy Clay, my father's mother, and the one person I know who's totally and unequivocally herself. After forty-two years as Mrs. Henry McCausland Clay of Mississippi, she really *is* a southern gentlewoman. But she's also half-Yankee and half-Irish, and she hasn't lost any of those qualities in her years as a company owner's wife. What's more, back in the dark ages of her youth, she'd insisted on a career instead of college. She'd been a photographer for a fashion magazine and had actually been caught overseas when World War II broke out. That's how she met Granddaddy, in England during the last year of the war, and when he came home from being a U.S. Army captain, she came with him as his wife.

She'd given up her career then, to run the old family homestead and the social side of the company's public relations, but she'd never lost her independent streak. I knew she'd understand the dilemma I was in.

"All right," Nannie said after I'd run through the whole mess at great emotional length. "As I understand it, the question is how to get you off the hook without hurting your mother or embarrassing both your parents. Is that your situation in a nutshell?"

I groaned. "Some nutshell! Where do I find an excuse my folks will believe? Fall off a horse and break my leg or something? I'd only have to go through the whole thing again next year!"

Nannie laughed. I love her laugh; it's deep and rich and what Daddy calls "decidedly bawdy." "You might just let your mother get the impression—without outright lying, mind you—that maybe there's hope for you as a debutante next year. A lot can happen in a year, you know."

"I couldn't change that much!" I said grimly.

Nannie laughed again. "Scratch the fall from the horse, Tori. You ride too well, and your mother would feel so sorry for you that she'd be quite capable of carting you to the ball in a wheelchair! How would you like to come with me on a Mediterranean cruise instead? Land knows your father's been pushing me to take one ever since your grandfather died."

I gasped. "I thought you said you wouldn't be caught dead on a cruise till you already had one foot in the grave!"

"I've changed my mind," Nannie said. "There are some things in the Mediterranean I would like to see again. I haven't been back there in over forty years, you know." I knew. My grandfather, who died last fall, had been a dear, but in his opinion anyone fortunate enough to live in "God's country," meaning Mississippi, had no reason ever to leave there. He'd made only two exceptions—military service during the war and visiting us in Texas.

"If I take your father's advice about a cruise," Nannie said practically, "maybe he'll stop pushing me to move to Texas. Not that I wouldn't like being near you all. But I really don't need looking after. I know I let your grandfather do it for years, but that was only because he got such a kick out of it. I didn't *need* it."

Like I said, I knew my grandmother would understand exactly how I felt. "What are you thinking of? Going back to your old career?" I teased.

There was a brief pause. "No," Nannie said. Just like that: abrupt, flat. I'd never heard her use that voice before. Then her tone changed again, and the laughter I loved came back. "No, what I'm thinking of right now is rescuing you, my child. So hang up the phone and let me call your father. I'll tell him this poor old lady needs your company to ease the trauma of a journey into her past. Actually, that won't be far from the truth."

Nannie always did have the skill I lacked of sticking to the truth but packaging it in palatable form. I laughed and hung up, feeling a whole lot better. And within three days Nannie had sold my parents on the cruise idea and booked our passage. Mama threw herself into fixing me up with cruise clothes instead of ball gowns. Daddy actually gave me a little talk about not taking shipboard romances too seriously. Both of them told me to look after my grandmother, because she was getting old, and wasn't used to being on her own, and might find this "pilgrimage into her youth" unsettling. Since Nannie's still in her sixties, and the most realistic person I know, I said "yes, ma'am" and "yes, sir" and otherwise kept my mouth shut.

All of which explains why, on the twenty-first of June, as Sue Hopper and the other debs back home were preparing to climb into their white ball gowns, I was whirling on the dance floor of the S.S. *Medici*, somewhere off the coast of North Africa, in a beautiful copper-colored dance dress, talking to Mr. Entwhistle, the nice retired New Englander who shared our table in the dining room, and trying to avoid C. D. Mackenzie.

I'd first bumped into C.D., literally, on the gangplank in New York. He was so loaded down with camera equipment, he hadn't been looking where he was going. Only a little taller than me, and thin, with thick glasses in front of eager blue eyes and a shock of orange-colored hair, he was a camera nut so enthusiastic he never shut up. He was also a total klutz, just finished with his first year of college and on a tour of Europe that would apparently consist mainly of bumming around and taking pictures. He'd gotten standby passage on the cruise ship for peanuts. From day one, he'd decided I was the Southern Belle he'd been looking for all his life, and he simply wouldn't let me alone. He'd even managed to wind up sitting with Nannie and me at the purser's table.

Fortunately, the music stopped just as C.D. came ramming his way across the dance floor. Mr. Entwhistle, catching my imploring look, steered me back to Nannie. We and the Entwhistles were sitting, on couch and easy chairs, on the little gallery that ringed the crowded dance floor with its nightclub tables. C.D., of course, barreled over, too, his face one broad grin and his camera rampant. At the sight of it, we all groaned.

"Just let me get a few more pictures of you guys," he pleaded. "After all, this is the last night we'll all be together." Nannie and I were leaving the cruise ship the next morning in Tangier, to spend a few days there before crossing over into Spain.

"I thought you used up all your film when we pulled away from Madeira yesterday," Nannie said dryly.

"The ship's shop is sold out, but I talked the ship's photographer into selling me some of his," C.D. said, unabashed. "I guess you don't know it, Mrs. Clay, but nothing can come between a real photographer and his quarry."

Nannie said, "Is that the truth?"—real southern—and I hid a grin. Our first night out, Nannie had absolutely forbidden me to tell C.D. about her own picture-taking past.

C.D. used up his flashbulbs snapping me, Nannie and me, Nannie and me and the Entwhistles, and all of us with the purser. Then he rewound his film and stashed it and the other equipment in his camera bag.

"I almost forgot," he said, pulling out a brown envelope. "You know those pictures the ship's photographer took of us at the dinner table tonight? They weren't supposed to be ready till tomorrow after you guys went ashore, but I talked him into developing them early and letting me have copies."

He spread the pictures out on the coffee table in front of us, and we all bent forward. There we all were—the Entwhistles, looking dignified; C.D., enthusiastic; me in my copper dress and the lace shawl I'd bought myself in Madeira; Nannie in her black chiffon with her coronet braids and the dramatic white streak in her hair.

"You photograph beautifully. I always look so severe," Mrs. Entwhistle was saying ruefully to Nannie, when C.D. gasped.

He was staring at one of the pictures, at Nannie's face rather than mine, and all at once his eyes swung up to hers. For an instant, for the first time since I'd known him, he was speechless. Then the words burst out. "You—you're *Nance O'Neill!*"

By instinct, my eyes swung to my grandmother, and I'll

never forget the mixture of emotions on her face. Shock. Embarrassed pride. And, unless I was totally wrong, a kind of fear.

For what seemed like several seconds, nobody moved. Then Mr. Entwhistle exclaimed, "By golly, you're right. I should have known! We met in England once," he said to Nannie. "Right before the end of the war. It was at a USO dance, and you were with an army captain, if I remember right. Somebody told me you were the girl who'd gotten those pictures of one of the Nazi bigshots having a secret meeting in Spain with one of Stalin's puppets. I remember I couldn't believe it, because you looked so young and pretty, kind of helpless. But my buddy produced a copy of *Stars and Stripes* that gave you credit, so I lost my bet." He laughed. "A lot of water's gone under the bridge since then. I kept thinking I knew you from somewhere, but I couldn't place you. By golly, Nance O'Neill!"

"It's been a long time," Nannie said in that flat voice I'd heard her use on the phone. "I'm Nancy Clay now. I never was a real photographer. That was just—something I fell into while I was trying to prove to my father I could make it on my own."

"You sure proved it!" C.D. said, hitching his chair in closer. He looked around at us, his eyes alight. "Do you know she got a Pulitzer Prize for that photograph? A girl straight out of high school, working for a fashion magazine, scooped the professional journalists and the military! Do you know that photograph's still held up in photography schools as an example of creative journalism?"

He stared at my grandmother the way up till now he'd gazed at me. "Ms. O'Neill, don't you know you're a legend? I've seen little photographs of you in the staff notes sections of old magazines. But nobody knows what's become of you in the past forty years." He looked around at the rest of us. "I wouldn't have guessed, if it weren't for this picture. It's the pose. And the angle of light. They show up her bone structure—and, of course, she's still wearing the same hairstyle. My gosh, Ms. O'Neill, do you realize what an honor it's been for me, sitting with you for the past week? And you never told us!"

"I'm Mrs. Clay," Nannie repeated. " 'Nance O'Neill' died a long time ago." She rose, smiling. "I hope you folks will forgive me. I've been getting a dreadful headache— probably all that champagne, and I still have last-minute packing to do! We'll see you all at breakfast to say good-bye?" She looked at me and said firmly, "Tori?"

"Yes, ma'am," I said, rising hastily. It was the only time she'd ever asked me to leave the dancing early. Come to think of it, it was the only time she'd left early herself. She looked pale. Dad was right, I thought as I followed her to our cabin. Memories of the past were coming back to her. But I didn't know then that they were opening a Pandora's box of unfinished business.

2 The sounds of luggage being bumped along the passage outside our cabin woke me early. I sat up and glanced out of our porthole, and all traces of sleep fled swiftly. The shoreline of North Africa was silhouetted against the dawn-red sky.

Nannie's bed was empty and her overnight bag sat on it, already tidily half-packed. We'd had to have all luggage, except what we'd carry ashore ourselves, packed and out in the corridor by midnight. Nannie herself stepped out of the tiny bathroom, in her dark jersey robe and a towel turban.

"You can have the shower now if you want," she said. "I'm going to order early breakfast in our stateroom. I'd like us to be among the first to disembark." Her voice was brisk, but her face, perhaps because of the navy robe, looked pale.

"Thanks, I showered last night." I was already pulling on the sundress I'd kept out to wear. "Okay with you if I go up on deck and watch us dock? And eat in the dining room this one last time?"

"Just be sure you come back in time to finish packing."

"Bet I'll have my whole bag packed in less time than it takes you to pack your makeup kit," I answered, grinning. The amount of cosmetics Nannie used to achieve her unmadeup look was a family joke. Nannie had been rumored to travel the world with just hairbrush, tooth-brush, and red lipstick in the past—but she didn't do it now if she didn't have to.

I gave my hair a hasty brushing and made for the door.

The red in the sky had faded to pale yellow when I reached the deck, and the faint breeze hinted of later heat. The water sparkled, and the rooftops of Tangier gleamed like pearls. Here and there a slender tower rose. Mina-rets—of course, Morocco was a Moslem country! I gazed, enchanted.

I half expected C.D., with camera, to bounce up behind me. But he didn't, and I was relieved. Having this little piece of the upper deck all to myself, this first look at Tangier, in its stillness, was so special. Gradually, the sky grew brighter and other people joined me, but the spell still lingered. Small boats, beetlelike beside the bulk of our ship, raced out to meet us. Slowly, with great dignity, we approached the wharf.

The ship's gong rang to announce breakfast, and I went inside. C.D. didn't appear in the dining room, either. Maybe we weren't going to get to say good-bye to him. Considering his big announcement of last night, maybe it was just as well, I decided. The Entwhistles kept asking me questions about "Nance O'Neill," and I decided Nannie had been smart to hide out in our cabin. My grand-mother the celebrity—who'd have thought it!

I excused myself as soon as I could and ran down to finish packing. Nannie was all ready to go ashore, wearing dark glasses and her big-brimmed sun hat. We did man-age to be among the first to leave the ship, but that wasn't till nearly ten A.M., what with all the customs and immigration formalities to comply with. Actually, we had a very easy time of it. Nannie smiled graciously at the customs men, and they peered into our suitcases at the top layer of clothes and waved us through. Finally we were down the gangplank, on a long, narrow wharf engulfed in a blanket of heat.

"Come on," Nannie said firmly, striding toward a bank of taxis at the far end of the wharf. Our porter followed her, luggage-laden. I tried to keep up with them, but it was hard. Too many sights and sounds distracted me. Smells, too—not all of them good. I felt as if I'd stepped into *The Arabian Nights*.

There were tawny-skinned peddlers, darkly handsome, hawking those curved brass knives called scimitars. Old ones with wispy beards and missing teeth, hawking coarsely woven Arab robes. Barefooted children determined to sell me goodness knows what and demanding "*Baksheesh!*" in shrill voices. I couldn't escape them; Nannie and the porter just kept walking through the wall of human flesh surrounding them, but I could not.

All at once a voice broke through the cacophony of sounds. A voice shouting, "Tori! Wait up!"

I spun around just in time for C.D., camera bags and all, to crash right into me.

"It's your own fault," C.D. said calmly, helping me gather up our assorted paraphernalia. "You shouldn't have left the boat so fast that I didn't get a chance to say good-bye. And you shouldn't let your camera *or* that dumb open-top purse flap around like that. Don't you know that's an open invitation to pickpockets, Victoria Jane?"

"I told you not to call me that, *Clarence*," I said icily,

regretting the way I'd let him talk me into comparing passports once on shipboard. But I'd succeeded in making him regret it, too, I noted with satisfaction. C.D.'s face had turned as red as his hair.

"Okay, you win," he said hastily. "Tori and C.D. it is, henceforth and forevermore."

"Good. Not that we're apt to run into each other, I suppose." C.D. was sailing with the ship on to Italy.

"You never know," C.D. said absently. "Look, Tori, about last night. I didn't mean to get carried away like that—you know, going on and on about meeting a living legend. I hope I didn't embarrass your grandmother."

"I don't think anybody could embarrass Nannie." I started to laugh. And then, abruptly, the image of Nannie's face as it had looked last night rose up in my memory. My smile died.

Fortunately, C.D. didn't notice. "Don't pay any attention to these kids, or you'll regret it," he advised, detaching two of them from my left leg. "Come on, I'll carry your junk to the taxi for you. I want to apologize to Nance O'Neill."

"Don't push your luck. She might throw something at you. If you really are having an attack of the guilts, send her a postcard when you get to Italy. Hotel Grande. I don't know the street address, but it's right outside the entrance to the old city. And address it to *Mrs. Henry McCausland Clay*," I said pointedly.

"Okay, I will. Here's your stuff. Hang on tight to it, remember?" C.D. gave me a grin, and a last wave, and vanished in the crowd. I plowed on to where Nannie and the cab were waiting, still feeling oddly out of place.

That sense of unreality lingered as we swept along the shore and pulled up before an enormous sprawl of white-washed stucco, all domes and lacework. The Hotel Grande—and grand it was, right down to the acres of Oriental carpeting in a lobby dripping with mosaic tiles and gilt.

We followed an army of porters down a ground-floor corridor. And then the assistant manager, who had insisted on personally escorting us, turned an enormous brass key in the middle of an enormous lock. The door swung open and even Nannie's celebrated poise deserted her. "My word!"

It wasn't a room; it was a whole suite—maybe a baby palace. "M'sieu Guillaume made clear that Madame must have our best accommodations," the assistant manager said. Mr. Guillaume was the local top gun from Grand-daddy's company, McCausland Industries. "Unfortunately, the Royal Suite is at the moment engaged by a person from the music industry. He is making a 'rock video.' This is the *Suite Ducale*—the Ducal Suite. I trust Madame will find it satisfactory."

"Quite," Nannie said, very grand, and winked at me when he wasn't looking. She shook hands with the assistant manager, got rid of the porters with some American dollar bills, and we were alone in our gilded splendor.

I kicked off my sandals and plopped down on a tooled-leather pouf. "Whew! Is Morocco all like this?"

"There are two extremes. This is one; you'll see plenty of the other." She moved, at the same quick pace she'd used on the wharf, from one room to another, as I followed, barefoot. Sitting room: red and gold brocade

14

walls, red and gold Persian rug, gold French furniture, and lots of brass. Floor-to-ceiling glass doors opening onto a private garden walled in more of those white-washed openwork cement blocks. The sound of brakes, horns, and screeching tires indicated a main road was just beyond the wrought-iron gate. Next to the sitting room, a small, square, high-ceilinged room all in blue and lime-green mosaic tile, with a hanging brass lantern and lime-green banquettes surrounding a low brass table.

"Moorish dining room," Nannie explained, barreling on into the smaller of the two bedrooms—pale blue brocade, and a bed that would not have looked chintzy in Versailles. Sue Hopper should see me now, I thought. My suitcases had been set down on brass racks, and there was a whole wall of closets and a marble bathroom with loads of counter space.

Nannie's bedroom could have stood in for a ballroom, with bathroom and dressing room to scale. They were white and gold. On the bureau stood a basket of orchids. "Good grief!" I exclaimed involuntarily.

"Good Guillaume, you mean. Tribute to the boss's widow, I suppose." Nannie flipped the envelope open, read the card, and dropped it in a drawer.

"Guillaume?"

"The same. He craves the honor of giving us a person-ally escorted tour of Tangier, and our presence this evening at some party. I gather it's grand; he's very vague about details." Nannie was already dialing his office on the very chichi phone. The conversation was half in French, half in English. She begged off the tour and accepted for the party, about which Guillaume was still being cagey. Maybe it's for that rock star, I thought hope-fully.

"Change your clothes, and I'll take you on my own per-sonally guided tour of the medina. That's the old shop-ping area. No jeans; better yet, no slacks at all, and no bare arms." Nannie vanished into her bathroom and a moment later I heard her shower running.

Nannie always lived at a fast pace, but this was hyper, even for her, and I wondered why. Maybe it was seeing Morocco again, after all these years. I could hear her pac-ing like a cat through the suite as I unpacked some of my clothes and changed into a long-sleeved cotton dress. But when I emerged from my room she looked much as always, calm and trim in a linen shift and one of her big-brimmed hats.

We went through the gate of our private garden into the street, which ran between the side of the hotel and the walls of the old city. And we stepped back in time.

That afternoon was a blurred montage of sights and sounds and smells. And tastes. Mint tea in tall glasses with silver handles. The outdoor food market, with fruits and vegetables set forth in exquisite piles, on shabby, dirty rugs, by veiled, black-robed women. Awninged butchers' stalls hung with fly-covered sheep carcasses, and live sheep and goats tied out back. Spice stalls. Beverage stalls, where sweetened fruit juices were sold from tall ceramic jugs. Shops built into the buildings of the old city, with doors standing open to entice passersby. Shops for brass-ware, shops for caftans, shops for jewelry.

I immediately wanted to bargain for a caftan, but Nannie insisted we wait for a special shop she knew. She kept trying to find shops she remembered, without success. Forty-five years is a very long time.

We turned a corner that Nannie found familiar, and were in a small open square. The begging children were everywhere. Music—thin, high, and sweet—came from the center of a ring of tourists. Nannie, who had been looking faintly drawn, suddenly smiled.

"Come on! You must see this."

The ring of tourists opened slightly to let us in. At its center an old man, turbaned, sat cross-legged on a filthy rug and played his pipe. Before him, a huge jar-shaped straw basket rocked with the swaying movements of its occupant. A cobra, huge, yellow-green, hypnotized—

I turned away hastily, breathing hard.

The far side of the square fascinated me much more. Those old, old buildings, one running into the other to become one unwindowed wall, with the dark blue doors, tight shut. Here and there, steep narrow stairs disappearing upward into shadows. And high on the wall, just as in cities back home, an advertising poster. The writing was in Arabic, but I could recognize the Coca-Cola bottle.

Against the wall, in a patch of sunlight, a veiled young woman in a shabby caftan cuddled a baby, while a barefoot, ragged toddler clung to her side. Up till now I'd been photographing tourist sites—when I remembered to. Now, almost by instinct, I lifted the camera hanging around my neck, squinted, and focused on the woman and her children.

I was snapping the shutter when I felt it—felt it so strongly that I literally recoiled. A wave—no, *waves*—of hate were rolling toward me inexorably . . . out of the

17

walls, out of the dust, out of eyes that suddenly seemed to be glaring at me from the shadows.

I stumbled, and my camera fell from my fingers, to dangle foolishly against my chest. I must have backed up, for when I bumped into someone I almost screamed.

It was Nannie. Her hand was grasping my arm; her voice was saying urgently into my ear, "Come on. *Quickly!*"

She marched me off down the wide street, at the heels of a large and well-organized group of German tourists. She didn't let go until we were outside the medina, back on the street leading to our own hotel. Nannie flagged the first empty cab and pushed me in.

"Nannie, what—"

"Not now," she said sharply. We rode in silence the few blocks to our hotel.

We went in through the main entrance, hurrying past the hotel staff, who bowed and scraped. We reached our suite, and Nannie unlocked the door as I stooped to pick up the folded newspaper that had been left outside. An English-language paper, I noticed vaguely, following my grandmother into our sitting room.

Nannie locked the door behind us and turned to me, and I noticed she looked as unnerved as I felt myself. "I'm sorry," she said to me. "I should have warned you."

"Warned me *what?*"

"This is a third-world country, and even if Tangier is a cosmopolitan city, many people are very . . . What I'm trying to say is, don't take pictures of the people, *ever*, unless you've asked permission. Particularly of the women. It's an invasion of their private space, it's against tradition, in some cases it violates old superstitions. Okay?"

When I blushed and nodded, she patted me on the shoulder. "Don't worry, there was no harm done. Now let's order some fruit juice and relax with the paper till it's time to get cleaned up for the party."

I nodded again and handed her the paper. Nannie flipped it open. All at once her face, already pale, looked like bleached bone.

This time it was I who reached for her. To steady her; to take the paper. And stare, and gasp.

Squarely in the middle of the front page was one of the pictures C.D. had shot last night. I hadn't seen finished photos, but I knew. Because there we all were, as we'd been on the gallery near the dance floor last evening—the Entwhistles, and me, and Nannie in her black chiffon. The caption read: Nance O'Neill, Famous American Photographer, Visiting in Tangier.

C.D. couldn't have gotten those pictures developed on board, because the photo lab was closed while the ship was docked. He'd gotten them done somewhere on shore. He'd taken this one to the newspaper, and gotten his "scoop," no matter how much he knew my grandmother would be offended.

Or was that the right word? My grandmother stood there, frozen, until the telephone's ring cut through us both like the whistling of a blade.

3 I scooped up the phone. Nannie simply stood there. "Hello?" I snapped.

"Tori, is that you?" C.D.'s exuberant voice bubbled over the wire. Somehow, I was not surprised. "Guess what? I've jumped ship. All the stuff you and your grandmother were telling me about Morocco got me hooked, so I decided to hang around awhile. Look, how about—"

"How about apologizing for ruining my grandmother's day?" I demanded harshly. "You have some nerve!"

"What? Oh. You've seen the paper."

"You bet we have, you rat."

"For pete's sake, your grandmother was a beginning photographer herself once, she'll understand," C.D. said unrepentantly. "I couldn't sit on a scoop like this; it would have been downright unethical!"

"Not to mention unprofitable."

"Oh, come on, Tori. Lighten up. Besides," C.D. added virtuously, "I'm going to spend the filthy lucre taking you two out for dinner tonight. That's why I called."

"We're busy."

C.D. drew his breath in sharply. "Wait a minute! Your grandmother's not really mad at me, is she?"

"Words," I said, "can't begin to describe it." I banged down the receiver.

By now the color was returning to Nannie's face, and

she was reading the rest of the paper intently. I ordered fruit juice from room service, and while we waited for it I reported C.D.'s side of the phone conversation. Nannie shook her head.

"I should have thought of it," she said ruefully. "I should have removed that roll of film from his camera bodily. Of course he sold it. He's right, it's probably just what I'd have done."

"There's no real harm done, is there?" I asked hopefully.

Nannie shrugged.

We didn't talk about C.D., or Nance O'Neill, anymore. The fruit juice came, accompanied by baklava and a bowl of pistachios. Nannie took hers with her into her posh bathroom for a long, leisurely soak in the marble tub. I finished unpacking and took great satisfaction in laying out my other new dance dress, white and silver lace. Somehow the one social amenity I never had trouble with was wearing really gorgeous clothes.

I climbed in and out of a shower, and spent a lot of time getting my hair (dark like Nannie's, but fortunately wavy like my mother's) to hang just right. And at last it was time to go to M. Guillaume's mysterious party.

Guillaume had sent a car for us, and it was waiting when Nannie and I, elegantly attired, crossed the lobby to the front door amid more of that staff bowing and scraping. "I wish they'd stop that," Nannie muttered beneath her breath as she flashed her gracious smile. "It's just because of who your grandfather was. It's embarrassing."

"Maybe," I whispered back, "it's because of who my *grandmother* used to be."

Nannie's lips tightened as she let the doorman assist her into the long black limo. I scrambled in before he could try the same maneuver on me. People, including the inevitable beggars, were watching from the sidewalk. Just as the doorman tried to close the car door, a flashbulb popped.

It wasn't C.D.; I knew that much because I took a fast look. It was a local. So not everybody here observes the no-photo rule, I thought. At least not where westerners were concerned!

"Please leave," Nannie ordered the driver crisply. And then, as the limo obediently swept away from the hotel, she turned to me.

"What you just said. I don't want to hear anything like that from you again, *ever*. Not directly, not by inference. The character you're trying to dredge up doesn't exist. I'm Mrs. Henry McCausland Clay. Please remember that."

I stared at her uncertainly. "Nannie, I'm sorry. I didn't mean—"

"I know you didn't. I'm just . . . making sure you understand." But I didn't, and as I continued to look at her in bewilderment, Nannie put one hand up to her brow. "I must be getting tired. Or old. Forgive me, Tori, it's probably my headache talking. Maybe your daddy's right, and coming back here after all these years has released too many ghosts."

She didn't say anything more for the rest of the drive to the villa where the party was being held.

How can I describe that villa, and that evening? Nannie had explained to me, before our trip, how entering a country with very different ways and values could make you feel like Alice through the looking-glass. I felt as if I'd stepped, not through a mirror, but through a clock. Time was all out of whack; I felt as if I were in the twelfth century (or earlier) and in the present, all at once. And as if time were playing tricks on me, racing fast and then standing still for moments without warning.

The villa was on the outskirts of the city, and it faced the sea. There were rocky cliffs along the shoreline, and tropical flowers foamed against them, neon colors in the moonlight. I don't know how large the villa was, but it was huge and, like almost every building I'd seen that day, a startling white. The doors were royal blue, and heavy, as though they'd been hacked out of great slabs of wood. There were lots of big black nailheads, and black wrought iron, and lots of openwork walls and grilles made of black wrought iron or white cement. There was a blue and gold awning canopy over the entryway, and beside it flaming torches taller than I am were mounted in iron brackets higher than my head. Beneath the torches stood—I didn't know what to call them—servants, guards in native dress complete with fezzes and wicked-looking antique weapons.

Other cars were arriving at the same time as ours. When one of the attendants opened the limo door and held an arm out to me, I copied the woman from the car ahead and climbed out grandly. Nannie followed, her usual cool well in place.

We went through the first set of gates, through the doorway, across a Moorish-tiled entry court with splashing fountain, and up a flight of stairs. Actually, we waited

23

in line on the stairs, with a lot of other guests, till the major domo at the top (fez, huge black mustache, enough gold braid to choke a horse) bawled out the names of each of us in turn.

"Madame Henri McCausland Clay. Mademoiselle Victoire Jeanne Clay." My full name sounded a lot better in French, I decided, than it did in English. Nannie winked at me as though she'd read my mind, and I grinned back, and we moved into the ballroom with the flow of traffic.

Pretty soon an important-looking Frenchman, in white tie and tails and medals, cut through the traffic toward us. "Ah, Madame Clay, *je suis enchanté.*"

"Monsieur Guillaume," Nannie returned smoothly. She knew him from trips he'd made to the States. He introduced his wife (red satin and diamonds), and Nannie introduced me. Before long, Mme. Guillaume had presented me with some young on-the-way-up men from Granddaddy's company, and aimed us toward the disco room, while bearing Nannie off in some more exalted direction.

If Sue Hopper and Buck could see me now, I thought between dances, coping with an assortment of roving dark glances, respectful-but-intimate voice tones, and wandering hands. I was just turning down the fourth offer of a personally escorted tour of the medina when I heard a voice behind me, in an all-too-exact parody, murmur, "Ah, Mademoiselle Victoire Jeanne. . . ."

C.D. In an ill-fitting tuxedo with a press badge pinned on haphazardly that read CLARENCE D. MacKENZIE, and, naturally, a camera.

"What are you doing, following us?" I demanded between my teeth.

"Sorry to disappoint you, but I'm covering a more important story," C.D. said blandly. He disengaged one of the roving male hands from my waistline, put his there instead, and steered me firmly off into an alcove. "Honest and truly, I didn't know you'd be here."

"What could be more important to you than making our lives miserable?"

"Hate to give another blow to your vanity, but I only did what any aspiring press photographer would do on finding out Argenteuil would be here tonight."

"Argen-*who*?"

"My gosh, don't you pay any attention to international politics? Argenteuil. General Jean-Pierre Argenteuil, God's gift to the French Chamber of Deputies and the French people. He's a war hero, ultraconservative, and incidentally a shoo-in for premier in this year's French elections. Didn't you know this party's in his honor?"

"I don't think even Nannie does," I said in a small voice. "I could swear Monsieur Guillaume never mentioned—"

"That's probably because this visit's real hush-hush," C.D. said, cheered by being able to educate me. "It's one of those unofficial butter-up-potential-allies things. Except some people, French and Arab and others, aren't too keen on the general, hence the secrecy. Did you see those armed guards outside?"

I shivered slightly. "If it's such a secret, how did *you* find out?"

C.D. shrugged. "I heard something from a guy I know."

"And just happened to get hold of a *Washington Post* press badge, I suppose."

C.D. grinned. "I got it off a guy I met in France last year. He owns a photo gallery near the medina. That's where I developed the photograph you got so mad about. Come to think of it, maybe you owe *me* an apology. My leaking your grandmother's secret got you both invited here tonight, didn't it?"

"For your information, *Mrs. Clay* and I were invited because Granddaddy's company does a lot of business here."

We were working up to a good Texas showdown, in spite of the audience now gathering in the alcove, when C.D. suddenly shut up in midsentence and turned red.

Nannie had arrived, holding her purse tightly and cutting through C.D.'s attempt at a disguised apology. "Hello, C.D. Tori, would you mind if we left? This frightful headache—"

She looked pale and strained. I nodded quickly and turned, and just at that moment our escape was cut off by the approach of M. Guillaume. He was beaming with importance and followed by a dark young Frenchman in military uniform.

"Ah, Madame Clay—"

The young Frenchman was one of General Argenteuil's aides-de-camp, who said General Argenteuil requested the honor of being presented to the illustrious Mme. Henri McCausland Clay, widow of the noted international industrialist.

It was pretty clear the noted industrialist's company

was going to get an international black eye, to M. Guillaume's alarm, at least, if Nannie didn't oblige. Nannie performed that company-wife trick I'd seen her use before, getting taller, getting calm, all traces of weariness and headache vanishing. On the aide-de-camp's arm, she swept through the aisle that cleared for them as M. Guillaume, C.D., and I followed on their tail.

By the time we reached the guest of honor, C.D. had whispered everything he thought I ought to know about him. In international politics, Argenteuil was a superstar. The Arabs liked him in spite of his being French. The U.S. liked him because he was a "bulwark against communism." The Europeans liked him because he thought the European Economic Community ought to have its own armaments against the Soviets instead of relying so much on America. The Russians respected him. He was on chummy terms with the king of Morocco, and with a lot of other North African leaders as well.

What C.D. didn't bother saying, what I could see for myself with one glance, was that Argenteuil was a charmer. A silver-bearded, deeply tanned, seventy-year-old golden boy. He lifted his right hand with one brief gesture as Nannie and her escort approached, and the rest of his entourage melted into the background as if by magic. Everything seemed to stand still. Everybody seemed diminished by Argenteuil's magnetism—everybody but my grandmother.

Nannie's head was high, her diamonds sparkled like the silver streak in her coronet braids, and her rose-pink chiffon swirled. And you could almost hear the electricity crackle in the room. Even C.D. was subdued by it, or so I thought, until the end of the aide-de-camp's ceremonial introduction: "Madame Henri McCausland Clay, I have the honor to present His Excellency, le Général Jean-Pierre Argenteuil."

For a moment the room was completely silent. Then Nannie held out her right hand to be kissed, murmuring with her most southern accent, "Charmed, I'm sure." And the general took her hand, and bent over it, and C.D.'s flash went off.

And all hell broke loose.

Two of the general's uniformed aides grabbed C.D.'s arms. Some of the dressed-up attendants from out front dashed up, only they didn't look humorous now with their guns held high. C.D.'s camera was confiscated and the film removed, then C.D. and camera were unceremoniously thrown out. Somewhere in the middle of all that, Nannie's silver high heel jabbed my instep sharply and I, too, was presented. We all made small talk.

Then one of the aides, a different one, took me to the refreshment table and tried to pump me about C.D. I replied, with what I hoped sounded like lighthearted amusement, that he was a shipboard acquaintance, a college student and aspiring photographer, and meant no harm. M. Guillaume came and rescued me, bringing one of the young company men his wife had introduced, and I was never so relieved to see anyone.

We went back into the ballroom, and we danced. I saw Nannie dancing with M. Guillaume, and soon after that I saw the general and his party leave. C.D. did not reappear. Nannie's headache seemed to have disappeared, too; in fact, I scarcely saw her for the rest of the party, which didn't break up until sometime after two. I caught glimpses of her, dancing or surrounded by animated groups of males, all ages, all smitten. I was having a very good time myself. In fact, I was practicing flirting in French.

At last, very late, M. Guillaume approached me, smiling. "Mademoiselle Victoire, Madame is waiting for you in the courtyard. She asked me to tell you your limousine is waiting."

Escorted by my phalanx of new admirers, I joined her. With other party guests, we made our way out into the torchlit street. The limo swept us home to a hotel that was quiet at this hour. The doorman had to make himself jump to attention, and the lobby was inhabited only by a yawning night clerk. "No pomp and circumstance, thank the Lord," Nannie murmured.

I giggled. "I'd say you coped with pomp and circumstance pretty well tonight. It sure cured your headache!" Nannie ignored that. We reached the suite, and she let us in.

"So how does it feel to be back in the singles scene again?" I asked mischievously. She ignored that, too, crossing directly into her bedroom without snapping on the sitting room lights. She went into her bathroom and flipped on the makeup lights that ringed the mirror, leaning forward intently to scan her reflection closely. The mirror gave back her aristocratic bone structure, and deepset eyes, the glittering diamonds and rose-pink chiffon.

"A far cry from wartime Nance O'Neill," my grandmother said, more to herself than to me.

"I suppose you wore fatigues and an army cap," I teased.

Nannie started as if she hadn't known I was there. "I was a fashion and society photographer, not a war correspondent, Tori. But I couldn't afford things like these at that age. Or get away with them."

I laughed. "I'll bet you got away with murder, even then."

I don't know how she would have answered that. She never got a chance. Because it was just at that moment that it started—a frantic hammering at the grilled doors leading to our private garden.

I jumped and cried out. One swift gesture from Nannie made me silent. With her other hand she snapped off the bathroom lights, then motioned me past her into the bedroom.

I saw her silver shoes glint as she kicked them off. Then, silent as a cat, she was sliding out of the bathroom and along the bedroom wall till she reached her nightstand, snatching a flashlight out of a half-open drawer. With the flashlight off but pointed like a gun, she slid in the same way into the sitting room, along the side wall, toward the garden doors, where a shadowy figure loomed.

Ignoring her signaled instruction, I crept behind her, plastering myself by instinct, as she had, against the wall. I don't know why I was so scared, especially since the knocks were growing fainter.

The figure silhouetted against the doors in the faint moonlight hadn't gone away. The knocks just grew softer, but they kept on. Erratic. Desperate. My mouth had the taste of salt, and my feet felt as if they were weighted with cement.

All at once, Nannie flicked on the flashlight, straight at the grilled glass doors. I heard her give a sharp exclamation. Then, suddenly, she was darting across the room, fumbling with the lock.

As she forced the doors open, the figure leaning against them toppled over. Toppled backward, twisting, so that his feet lay inside the sill but the great bulk of his body lay outside, on the ground cover, on its back.

As I ran over, Nannie's flashlight pointed downward, straight at the distorted face.

The man's face was writhing, as the bulky figure itself writhed, as if trying desperately to force words out.

Suddenly, there was no more writhing, just a terrible stillness that extended to my grandmother and me. Suddenly, time stood still.

"Nannie, he's *dead!*" I gasped.

4 My grandmother's right arm made a sharp slashing gesture, commanding me to silence. Her left arm swept her chiffon skirts up to her hips. She knelt in the garden, incongruous in her shoeless feet and pale panty hose, and her right hand, still in its long evening glove, felt the side of the man's neck, right beneath the jawbone.

Feeling for the pulse in the main artery, a corner of my mind said mechanically. How does she know about that? From TV cop shows, the same way I do, probably.

Nannie nodded without turning, one sharp nod. Yes, the man was dead. My mind said, Go telephone for help, but my feet stood there, still immobilized by fear. It may have been seconds, it may have been minutes, and all the time my grandmother knelt there in the walled garden, surrounded by her clouds of rose chiffon, and her slim gloved hands explored the stranger's body.

She's looking for heart medicine, I thought, my throat catching. Granddaddy had died of a heart attack, at home, while shaving. And then I realized she wasn't just searching the stranger's pockets. She was patting him down. Under his arms, down his sides, around his waist and hips and even his lower legs. I heard her give a soft exclamation, and then her hands came out from the back pockets.

They were not holding medicine. They held a wallet. Nannie thrust it down the front of her dress and stood, still holding her skirts carefully off the earth. "Get my slippers," she ordered in a whisper, and somehow I made my legs move and obeyed. I set the slippers, just as her imperious head jerk ordered, right inside the threshold, and Nannie stepped into them. Then, as fast as a jackrabbit running from a hunter, she ran into her bathroom with me at her heels, shut the door behind us, and flipped on the light switch.

The light, coming so suddenly, almost blinded me, and our reflection in the mirror made me giggle nervously. Me, ghost-white, still in my white and silver dress, gasping for breath. Nannie taut, the diamonds heaving at her throat. Nannie's hands, dumping out the contents of the dead man's wallet on the marble counter.

"Keep quiet," Nannie whispered, so low I could scarcely hear. Her gloved fingers were examining the few objects the wallet contained. Five shabby bank notes. A half-used packet of matches. Some of the small coins called dirhams. An international driver's license with the dead man's photo. Name: Hector Alvarez. Age: 63. Nationality: Spanish. Residence: Algiers, c/o Spanish Consulate. Hair: black. Eyes: brown. Identifying marks: none.

There was nothing personal in the wallet at all. And there had been nothing else, not even keys or a handkerchief, in any of those pockets.

"Nannie, don't we have to call the police—"

"In a minute." Nannie replaced the wallet's contents and snapped off the bathroom lights. Then she flashed back to the garden doors and, stepping out of her slippers, replaced the wallet in the man's back pocket.

The man. I couldn't bring myself to think of him as *the corpse*. Or as a person named Mr. Alvarez.

All at once I swayed. "Don't you dare faint!" Nannie's command, sensed more than spoken, stopped me. I shook my head and forced myself to straighten.

Nannie was out in the garden, behind the dead man's head. Her hands, the hands I was used to seeing holding a horse's reins or pouring coffee, were hooked in the corpse's armpits. Little by little, with a strength I hadn't known she had, she was dragging it backward, farther onto the vinelike ground cover that kept the earth beneath from showing footprints.

Hector Alvarez's booted heels bumped over the threshold of the doorway, out into the garden, onto the greenery. Swiftly, Nannie tidied his clothes so they didn't show the body had been moved. She reached out a hand to me and, as if I'd read her mind, I handed her a tissue from my pocket. Nannie wiped the soles of the shabby boots and then, her eyes squinting with concentration, wiped the doorsill and, with a second tissue, the tiled floor. Then she closed the doors, locked them, and shut the curtains. Like a sleepwalker, she went back to the bathroom and flushed the tissues down the toilet.

Then she flipped the lights on in the suite, and the shock of them broke the spell. My legs could move again, and they moved me to the phone. Within seconds the night clerk's sleepy voice was sounding. *"Allo? Bonsoir? Ici le commissaire. . . ."*

Nannie snatched the phone out of my fingers. "Mrs. Clay, in *Suite Ducale*. I think there is a prowler in our private garden. A sound woke me. No, the door is closed and locked, and the curtains drawn. Please check from outside; my granddaughter is asleep and I don't wish to alarm her. Thank you." She hung up.

I stared at her. "Nannie, *why?*"

Nannie reached out and touched my face. "Darling, listen. Quickly. We're in a third-world country, not the U.S.A. I'm responsible for you, and I'm not going to let you get caught up in a North African police investigation. We aren't involved in this. But do you think anybody will believe that? I'm your granddaddy's widow, and a major stockholder in McCausland Industries. We could be an open target—"

I started to laugh hysterically. "You mean good ol' Monsieur Guillaume won't think having a man die in your garden is good for the company's public image!"

Nannie slapped me, hard. I gasped, and her gloved fingers touched the tingling spot gently. "Tori, I'm sorry. You must undress, and get in bed, and stay there. Quickly! I'll explain tomorrow." She was already stripping off her evening gown, and I followed her example.

By the time we heard footsteps outside the garden wall, we were already in our beds.

I heard the outer gate creak and footsteps coming closer, and I saw moving patterns of lights from flashlights. Footsteps receded, and soon more, official-sounding footsteps came. And an ambulance—even in Africa there was no mistaking the siren and the flashing lights. I could hear the lock on our door to the garden being tried. And then—silence.

After a long while I crept out of bed and into Nannie's

bedroom. She was sleeping. She lay so still, her hair in two braids down across her shoulders. There were deep shadows under her closed eyes, and her breath came in the even sounds of sleep. I went back to my own bed, and pulled the coverlet up over my head, and shivered.

No one bothered us. I lay there, and lay there, and those scenes in the garden kept rising up like a nightmare behind my eyes. The figure, looming. That hammering, so desperate, growing fainter. Our straight-out-of-TV reactions—thank goodness for those long happy hours I'd spent watching detective shows with Nannie and Granddaddy! And the look on Nannie's face when she'd stared down at the dead man's distorted face.

Almost as if she'd recognized him. It was crazy, but that's the way it seemed. Just like some other time, when I'd seen my grandmother look straight at someone, and go still—I searched my memory, but the incident escaped me.

Maybe it wasn't so crazy at that. Nannie'd met a lot of people in her sixty-five years. After all, she'd been Granddaddy's official hostess. . . . No, M. Guillaume wouldn't have liked any of this at all. *Not* the proper reception to Tangier for the owner's widow. But it was all right. Nannie had shown no recognition at all when she'd read Alvarez's driver's license. There must have just been some resemblance. And she'd acted so swiftly, just as Granddaddy would have done, so we weren't involved.

But the pictures kept haunting me as I went to sleep.

I didn't wake till eight. Nannie came into my bedroom, followed by a maid carrying a breakfast tray. "Tori, I'm so sorry, but you must eat quickly and get dressed. The manager has sent word the police want to speak to us, and they'll be here soon. There was a prowler outside our room last night."

"A prowler?" My eyes asked urgent questions, and hers answered, but she couldn't speak freely, not with the maid still there.

Nannie shrugged delicately. "I'm sorry, that's all I can tell you. I heard noises after you went to sleep, and I phoned the desk. I don't know any more."

Following her lead, I nodded and kept my mouth shut. I showered while the maid set out my breakfast on a little table. Nannie sat with me, drinking coffee while I ate. We didn't talk, for the maid was cleaning in the other rooms. As we heard the sound of the vacuum cleaner, Nannie's eyes met mine. Any traces of Mr. Alvarez's fall across our threshold were being whisked away.

The police came just as the maid was finishing. An officer in an elaborate uniform, and his subordinate, introduced with much formality by the hotel manager. My French wasn't up to everything that was being said, but I could tell the manager was making the point that Mme. Henri McCausland Clay was a big wheel. The policemen, like most men when they meet Nannie, soon fell all over themselves to be ingratiating.

"So sorry to trouble you . . . most fortunate that you telephoned. Alas, if we had been summoned sooner . . ." The officer's glance at the manager was anything but polite. I gathered the police felt that if the hotel staff hadn't poked around on their own, the prowler's life might have been saved.

Only they didn't think he was a prowler.

"A heart attack? Oh, how sad." Tears glistened in Nannie's eyes. "He must have stumbled to the nearest lighted door in search of help. If only I'd opened the door instead of being frightened and calling the front desk. Not that I know cardiopulmonary resuscitation. I swore I'd learn it after my husband was stricken, but I never have."

"He seemed to have died quickly," the younger policeman offered eagerly, earning a rebuking look from his superior. *Quickly*—the memory of that writhing face rose up in me, and I pressed my hand hard against my mouth.

"His name was Hector Alvarez," the officer said. "Is it known to you, madame? Here is his photograph." It was the one from the driver's license, enlarged. Nannie looked at it with thoughtful coolness.

"No," she said slowly. "No, I've never heard of this man before."

"Perhaps he knew you. He is a small wholesaler, according to the Spanish authorities. He buys from craftspeople and sells to merchants."

"What we would call a jobber. No, *M'sieu l'Inspecteur*, I am sorry. My husband's company is very large, it never deals with jobbers, as Monsieur Guillaume, the head of the Tangier office, can assure you. And my husband and I never traveled in Tangier."

"Forgive me, but Madame herself has been here. This Alvarez may have seen the photograph in the newspaper yesterday, and come to seek you. For assuredly, there is no reason to suspect he entered your garden for criminal purposes."

Nannie became her most regal. "It is more than forty years since I have been here. And I have never known a

Hector Alvarez, here or elsewhere. The man must have mistaken the entrance. I understand there is a rock star staying in the next suite. He may have wished an autograph."

"Or, as you said, madame, he may have been suddenly stricken and sought aid from the nearest lighted doorway."

Amid considerable ceremony, the police and the manager finally took their leave.

By now Nannie and I were exhausted. Nannie's face was gray behind its careful makeup, and the reality of what Daddy had said to me before I left home hit me. *Your grandmother isn't really as young as she thinks she is. She needs you to look after her, Tori.* So far, I thought guiltily, it had been Nannie who'd been looking after me.

"Come on, Nan," I said briskly. "Let's go have lunch somewhere and shop for caftans."

Nannie roused herself. "You're right. If we sit around here, we're both going to get morbid. And once this story hits the papers, we'll be haunted by a redheaded roving photographer! Let's go."

We ate lunch in a French restaurant and then we hit the shops. This time we stuck to the upscale area on either side of the entrance to the medina. Guided by Nannie, I bought an embroidered black cotton caftan and silver filigree earrings. Nannie bought us both some tooled Moroccan leather slippers with turned-up toes. I also bought film, and I took pictures, but carefully, of scenes Nannie said were okay and of shopkeepers and beggars who were delighted to pose in exchange for coins. We'd stopped at a bank to change money, and mine was going fast. Within two hours I had only a few dollars worth left of the traveler's check I'd cashed.

"We ought to start thinking about getting back," Nannie said, running her hand across her eyes. Then she frowned. "No, wait. Let's just go down this side street first. It seems familiar."

We turned down a narrow side street just by the entrance to the old city, and found it choked with food stalls and the shops of artisans. It was not the first street Nannie'd thought looked familiar, but turned out not to be. Nannie kept looking tireder, and the street kept getting smellier, what with the open sewer and the goats who were adding their own distinctive smell to the odor of roasting meat.

"I don't know about you, but I've had enough of this," I said frankly. "Let me use up the rest of this roll of film on this little kid, and then let's go."

Nannie nodded. I showed my camera to the little boy, who'd been pestering me to take his picture, his huge eyes pleading. He happily ran over to a nearby shop to pose against the fly-specked windows.

His choice of a background wasn't very good, I thought with amusement; the shop was closed, its blinds drawn, and some locals were killing time nearby. I took the picture and gave the kid my last three dirhams, and he ran off. Then I took the camera, which was getting heavy, off my neck, rewound the film, and stashed the camera in my bag.

"You want to change film?" Nannie asked. I shook my head.

"Let's go someplace cool and quiet and I can do it there. Preferably someplace that sells tea or lemonade."

So we stopped at a teahouse, only I didn't bother changing film. I was so tired that Nannie took one look at me, once we were sitting down, and removed the camera from me firmly. "I'll put this in my purse. You have enough to carry with all our shopping." I had one of those string shopping bags, a paper one from the caftan shop, and a lot of small bundles stuffed in my oversized handbag.

We stepped out into the late afternoon sunlight, arm in arm. "The weary leading the weary," Nannie said, chuckling. "Now we just need to pick up some toothpaste, and we can go home." Nannie had her purse over her arm, held tight along with one parcel. And I had all my assorted junk hanging heavily from my left arm.

My left arm's always been kind of weak, ever since the time I fell off a horse right on it. Maybe that's why I wasn't more careful. I didn't know what was happening till I felt the tug of the leather strap against my shoulder.

Somebody was trying to steal my bag.

"*No!*" I shouted, and hung on tight, remembering too late C.D.'s warning. Something shoved me, and I went sprawling amid a cascade of falling bundles. I hung on to the handbag's strap for dear life.

And then, in spite of everything, I started to laugh. For there, like something out of a comic strip, came C.D.

He charged up the street, shouting, "Stop, you thief!" and a lot of gutter French.

I felt a slight scratch and a sudden lightening of pressure on my shoulder. And then I was sitting there in the dust, gazing in disbelief at a thin trickle of blood coming from the small slash in my upper arm. C.D. charged through the mob of urchins on the tail of the pickpocket who'd slashed the strap of my bag in half and run off free.

5 Nannie knelt beside me quickly. A shopkeeper rushed out, offering first aid. Nannie shook her head. "It's just a scratch. We'll take care of it when we get back to the hotel. I hope you've had a tetanus shot," she said. I nodded.

C.D. returned, panting. "Here's your bag. I told you to be more careful! The guy dropped it in the street as soon as he knew I was after him. You'd better look and see what's gone."

We transferred ourselves over to the ledge of a white-washed planter, and C.D. held the audience off while I checked my purse. "My wallet's gone."

"Passport?" C.D. said instantly. Nannie shook her head.

"Those are locked in a safe place." She meant our private safe deposit box at the hotel. "What's missing, Tori?"

"Just some snapshots and stuff that were in the wallet. I emptied out most of the junk, and my driver's license, before I left home. A few dollars worth of money. And some rolls of film."

"What about your camera?" C.D. asked.

I shook my head.

"I think," Nannie said, "it's time we went back to the hotel."

"I'll get a cab," C.D. said promptly, and Nannie nodded gratefully. While he was gone, Nannie gave me stern lessons in how to carry handbags in areas frequented by pickpockets. C.D. returned, in the front seat of a cab. He jumped out and helped us carefully into the backseat, then climbed in again.

"No way," he said when Nannie demurred, "am I letting you go home alone. Want me to report this to the police for you, Tori?"

Nannie and I exchanged glances. "No, thanks," I said primly.

"If you change your mind, remember I was a witness. Not that it would do much good, probably," C.D. added. "From what I hear, in tourist traps like this, when something's gone, it's gone. The guy was probably after money and credit cards. And your passport. U.S. passports are worth something on the black market. One of these kids in the street probably snatched the film."

"It won't be worth anything. I'm a lousy photographer," I said.

"Even so, it's a shame for you two to have a scare like that. I guess you're not much used to crime and violence," C.D. said gallantly.

If you only knew, I thought hysterically. I didn't dare look in my grandmother's direction.

C.D. was a lifesaver. How he'd gotten the cab I had no idea, for the streets were jammed and there were few cabs around. He wasn't being a pest, either; he was more quiet than I'd ever seen him. When we reached the hotel he beat the doorman to help us out, paid off cab and doorman, and ordered the concierge to send tea to our room.

He walked us to our very door, and when Nannie, struck by his courtesy, invited him inside, he refused.

"You don't need me, you need peace and quiet." He hesitated, reddening slightly. "Look, Mrs. Clay, I meant what I said to Tori on the phone yesterday. I'm sorry if that picture embarrassed you. And I *would* like to take you out to dinner to apologize, if you're up to it. After all, I owe you one."

"You owe me a good deal more than one, young man," Nannie said crisply. Then she smiled. "After this afternoon, I think the account's marked *paid*. If it's all right with Tori, you come to dinner with us. My treat. At a special Moroccan restaurant I know."

C.D. looked at me, and I nodded. His face split into a broad grin. "All *right!*" he said, and did some kind of broad jump in the hall, and took off.

Nannie looked after him. "I wonder if that Peter Pan will ever grow up. He showed some definite signs of it today, I'll grant him that."

"Nannie? Do you think he knows about last night?"

"Do you think he could have kept his mouth shut if he did?" Nannie asked back. "I have a feeling the story hasn't made the papers at all. The fine Machiavellian hand of Guillaume, I just bet."

The English-language afternoon paper lay folded outside our door, and we carried it inside with us. Nannie was right. There wasn't a word anywhere about Hector Alvarez and his fatal heart attack—not even in the obituaries.

Nannie dropped the newspaper into the wastebasket.

"Let's go swimming," she said abruptly. "If we sit around here, I'll jump out of my skin."

I went to my room and put on my blue bikini, and Nannie put on her black and scarlet suit and a scarlet caftan. By that time the tea C.D. had ordered had arrived, and we ate and drank gratefully. Then I put on a terry-cloth coverup, and we walked to the hotel pool.

Nannie was right; this was a good idea. The pool occupied an inner court off the back area of the lobby, and was complete with all the requirements of the rich and famous. There were special lockers for each room, accessible only by special keys given to the guests. There was a shallow pool for children. There was a whirlpool. There were umbrella tables, and every variety of chaise longue. An international assortment of all ages with nothing in common but money and gold jewelry lolled and swam. The rock star was holding court with his entourage on the far side of the pool. I recognized him, but I wasn't as excited as I would have been a few days earlier. Nannie and I locked our handbags in our special lockers and lay down on chaises, and I tried not to think.

"What we need is exercise," Nannie's voice came at last. She pulled on a bathing cap and dove into the pool. I followed. Nannie was right; after several brisk laps I did feel better. The trouble with me is I've seen too many old movies on TV, I thought, cheered. After all, I'd come to Europe and Africa for adventure!

And to look after Nannie. I hadn't done so hot a job of that so far, had I? Not that I could think of any more I could have done.

"We'd better start getting dressed," Nannie said at last,

reluctantly. "That boy will be here before we know it." Nannie retrieved her handbag, but I left mine in the outside locker. There was nothing of value in it anymore except the camera, which Nannie'd returned to me. Considering what had happened at our suite last night, I thought the camera was safer in the locker than in my room.

"We never did buy that toothpaste," I remembered as we headed for the suite.

"We'll get it tomorrow. Bicarb of soda was good enough when I was young, and when you were, too," Nannie answered. "Remember summer camp?"

"Don't remind me. Snakes and bugs!"

Nannie laughed and disappeared into her shower. I followed her example. One of the luxuries I'd be real happy to get used to, I thought, toweling myself dry, is these individual dressing-room baths! Back home Daddy was always yelling about my taking too much time in the main bathroom, because he thought the light was better there for shaving than in the dinky half bath that was attached to the master bedroom.

Not that I really needed anything half as palatial as this. A little TV on a wall shelf angled so you could watch it from the bathtub *and* from the throne! A telephone on the marble counter, and another at the tub. And a washbowl/dressing counter with its yards of marble, and yards of three-way mirrors, and all those drawers for cosmetics I didn't use! I just had my toothbrush and shampoo, comb and brush, jumbled together in the top drawer. There wasn't even any toothpaste, just that dinky box of baking soda I shared with Nannie.

Maybe I ought to try out some cosmetics now that I was in the exotic tropics. I wonder how I'd look in that kohl eyeliner, I thought, peering at my reflection. Maybe I'd buy some when I bought the toothpaste. Tonight C.D. would just have to take me as plain old unvarnished Tori.

I'd better hurry or he'd be taking me as plain old undressed Tori. I hurried into bra and panties and pulled on my terry-cloth coverup. I should have hung the new caftan in the bathroom while I showered, I realized. Oh, well, I'd wear it, creases and all. I got it out, and the new silver earrings, and went into Nannie's room to get my pair of Moroccan slippers. "Almost ready?" Nannie asked, braiding up her hair. She was already dressed.

"Almost. Come in for me when you're ready."

I padded back to the bathroom in the new slippers, and stared at myself hard in the mirror. I didn't look like somebody who'd found a body last night and been mugged today. I still looked like an average American girl, a Texas one, kind of outdoorsy. Same dark hair that curled just enough without my doing anything. Same gray-green eyes like Mother's. Same olive skin, just a little more sunburned. That was comforting, since I didn't *feel* as if I was the same person I'd been a few days before. I reached for the baby oil bottle and dabbed some on.

I decided that I would definitely try the kohl eyeliner. Usually I avoided makeup because I hated the idea of wearing a false face. But maybe the faces we all were born with were false in a way, not really us. Right now mine didn't reflect anything that had happened to me recently. C.D. had said something like that once, on shipboard, regretting his comically orange hair and look of eagerness.

That wasn't him, he'd said, any more than Clarence Derwent, the name his mom and dad had stuck him with, was really him.

The only person I knew who really was exactly what she seemed was Nannie. And even she kept Nance O'Neill a secret from all but family.

I realized I'd been standing there, looking at my reflection, for several minutes. Maybe I'd been out in the sun too much today, I thought, stifling a giggle.

One thing was for sure: that wavy hair of mine needed brushing. I pulled open the pitifully underused drawer I kept my comb and brush in.

I screamed.

The drawer wasn't mostly empty anymore. A *thing* was coiled inside, right over the hairbrush, slim and green and deadly. As the drawer slid out it shot up, as the cobra in the marketplace had shot up. Rearing, swaying gently, its forked tongue avid.

I screamed again, and my saliva was dry and salty in my mouth. I dared not move.

The snake stared at me, and I stared back. My left hand still clutched the bottle of baby oil. It slid from my fingers and crashed to the marble floor.

And then, miraculously, Nannie was there behind me.

"*Sing!*" she ordered. "Quickly! Anything!"

Hoarsely, I started singing the first thing that came to mind. "Happy birthday to you. . . . Happy birthday to you. . . ."

Behind the swaying horror of the snake I saw Nannie's mirrored reflection disappear, reappear with a tightly rolled newspaper in her hand.

"Tori, listen to me," she said in a low, even voice. "Keep singing till you're outside the door and it's slammed shut!" I nodded. Nannie edged in and then, suddenly, grabbed me by one elbow and flung me toward the door.

The snake reared and darted. I sang loudly. "Happy birthday to youuuuu!"

The song seemed to calm the snake. It swayed with the rhythm. I edged toward the door. Once I was past her, Nannie lunged in like a fencer. The roll of newspaper knocked the snake down toward the drawer.

Except that as the paper struck, so did the snake. It reared again, its tongue lashed out, and the teeth sank into Nannie's arm.

I didn't dare scream.

Nannie reeled, but she kept on striking with the roll of paper. The snake fell back into the drawer, and she slammed the drawer shut and leaned against it, holding tight to her other arm above the bite point.

"Get help!" she ordered hoarsely.

I didn't want to leave her, but I had to.

6 I never thought of the phone. I don't know why, except maybe I was scared to stay in the suite with the snake. I ran into the corridor, in my underwear and swimsuit coverup, shouting for help.

The corridor was so long, and there was no one in it. And then, with the inevitability of a bad movie, C.D. was there, running toward me, catching me. "What the hell's going on?" he demanded.

I fought free. "Don't stop me! Nannie—there was a snake in the suite—she's hurt—"

C.D. let go of me then, so fast I almost fell. He streaked down the corridor toward the lobby, yelling "*Au secours!*"

The assistant manager appeared, and C.D. grabbed him. "Ducal Suite—Mrs. Clay's been bitten by a snake!"

The lobby erupted into action. The desk clerk got on the phone to call an ambulance. The head bellman grabbed a forked rod and a net out of the baggage room. He, the assistant manager, the manager, and C.D. all took off for the Ducal Suite at top speed.

I tried to keep up with them, but I couldn't. My lungs were hurting, and I was gasping for breath, bent double. My coverup was falling off. A lady in one of those gray outer caftans pulled hers off, revealing a jeweled satin dress beneath, and wrapped the caftan around me. I gabbled my thanks and kept on trying to run.

I neared the suite just as the first of the rescue team was trying to get in. I'd let the door slam shut and lock behind me. The head bellman produced a key and used it.

Inside, everything looked so ordinary and was so still. "The smaller bathroom!" I shouted, and they stormed through the suite and opened the bathroom door cautiously.

Nannie was still where I'd left her, holding the drawer jammed shut with her derrière and clutching her arm. She looked gray and weak. The head bellman took in the situation in one glance and took over. He snapped orders in a language I didn't understand, and the assistant manager got a chair and wedged it beneath the drawer handle. He nodded at C.D., who eased Nannie away gently. He and the manager half carried her out of the bathroom.

The assistant manager took the net and, at the head bellman's signal, pulled the chair out cautiously. The drawer came with it—one inch, two—

The snake shot up as it had before, its mouth an evil grin.

Snap! The bellman lunged, pinning the snake against the marble counter, the forked rod holding it just at the base of the flat green head. The rest of the iridescent green body thrashed.

Snap! A knife, produced out of nowhere, flashed. The head was severed. It dropped to the floor like a discolored thumb.

The rest of the snake's body lay, half on the counter, half in the drawer, still thrashing. Gradually, the thrashings grew slower, feebler, just like the knocking and the writhing of the man last night—

I must have fainted for a minute. All I knew was the room grew dark. And then C.D.'s arms were around me, and he was saying anxiously, "Good Lord, Tori, don't give up now! Everything's going to be all right!"

He was carrying me across the room and laying me down on my own bed, and I'd never thought that he could be so gentle.

"Nannie . . ." I whispered.

"She'll be okay. They're taking her to the hospital now—over her protests, I might add."

"I want to go with her—"

"Not till you're in good enough shape not to disgrace the family." C.D. held a glass to my lips. "Drink this."

I took a swallow and choked as fire ran down my throat. "Brandy," C.D. said. "Courtesy of the manager." An ambulance siren shrieked outside our garden, and he put a hand on my arm as I struggled to get up. "They can't wait for you; they have to get her to the hospital fast. I'll take you as soon as you're okay."

I sat up, forcing myself to breathe slowly. "I'm okay."

"Sure?"

"I have to go with her, don't you understand?" I stood up, dizzily, and started for the door.

"I'd suggest you put some clothes on first," C.D. said dryly. He picked up the phone and arranged to have a cab come for us, and I grabbed a dress and ducked into Nannie's room to put it on. I couldn't face reentering the bathroom.

As I pulled off the borrowed caftan and then my terry-cloth coverup, my key ring fell out of the coverup pocket. I hastily stuffed it in the pocket of my dress.

I don't know what I'd have done without C.D. He waved off my suggestion that I needed to get some money from my handbag, locked up the suite, and guided me down the corridor to the waiting car. He took over, with surprisingly good French, at the hospital, and succeeded in getting me admitted to Nannie's bedside in intensive care, although he himself had to remain outside.

Nannie still looked gray, and old—she hadn't had a chance to put her makeup on before it all had happened. But her eyes burned like fire. I held her left hand because her right arm was all done up in bandages. "Don't try to talk."

"Don't try to stop me," Nannie whispered through dry lips. "Doctors—won't let me out—"

"They want to keep you a few days, till they're sure you're all right. Don't worry, Nannie. They say you're doing fine." That was a very optimistic version of what they'd told me, but I had to say it.

Nannie's fingers tightened on mine. "Tori, *listen*—call Guillaume. Tell him I say you're to stay with him."

"Nannie, that's not necessary—"

"You don't understand—I can't tell you—"

"It is time for you to leave, mademoiselle," a starched nurse interrupted.

Nannie's eyes bored into mine. "Promise."

So I promised, though I didn't intend to keep my word. I said I'd be back first thing in the morning, and I went. C.D. found a cab and directed it to the Hotel Grande, and climbed in with me. He didn't try to talk during the ride, and I was glad, for my mind was racing.

It was all very well for the hotel manager to say, as he'd done repeatedly, that snakes were everywhere in Morocco and that this one must have come in from the garden. I didn't believe him.

That bathroom drawer had been shut. The snake had been inside it, and it had been *my* drawer.

It had been my purse somebody'd tried to steal, with my film and presumably my camera inside. It had been I who'd provoked those waves of hate yesterday in the medina, when I'd snapped pictures. Nannie'd told me taking unauthorized photographs was dangerous, and look at everything that had happened since. My purse snatched, and my film stolen. The snake in my drawer. And last night, someone pounding on our door, and dying.

He could have been trying to break in. Or he could have been trying to tell us something—the image of that distorted face, and the lips moving, rose vividly. We'd never know. He was dead. I didn't believe that was coincidence, and I knew quite suddenly and sharply that Nannie didn't think so, either.

What on earth could I have photographed to get us into so much trouble?

What should I do about my suspicions?

Suppose Nannie died?

I came to with a start to realize the taxi had stopped, and C.D. was shaking me gently. "Tori, you're home."

The doorman opened the taxi door and C.D. helped me out. "I'm coming in with you," C.D. said. I nodded gratefully.

We went into the lobby, and the manager was there, waiting for me. "Madame Clay, how is she? I trust there is not going to be any trouble—"

I couldn't help myself. "She's doing fine, or she'd better be! Hotel Grande! It's some grand hotel if guests don't have protection against intruders—"

The manager's eyebrows shot up. "Mademoiselle! All the world knows snakes are common in North Africa! That is why there is a plain warning in all the rooms not to leave unscreened doorways open. Surely Madame Clay, having been in this country some years ago, knew that. If Mademoiselle was so careless as to have ignored the proper precautions—"

"*I didn't*—"

C.D. gripped my wrist, hard. Just in time. I hadn't been starting to say I hadn't left the door open. I'd been about to blurt out I hadn't meant *snake* when I'd said *intruder*. But every instinct warned me I should keep my mouth shut.

For now.

"I hope the snake has been removed from Miss Clay's suite," C.D. said icily. The manager nodded. C.D. steered me down the corridor, took the key ring from my trembling fingers, and unlocked the door.

We stepped inside, and I started to laugh. Wildly. Crazily. Because once again I'd stepped into a TV scene.

The room had been trashed. Totally and completely.

C.D. swore under his breath. He shut and locked the door and stood behind me, one hand on my shoulder, and we looked around. The cushions had been yanked from the furniture, their covers unzipped and half pulled off.

Pictures were askew or off the wall. Drawers were pulled out and their contents dumped. Even flowers in flowerpots had been jerked out and lay, wilting. In my bathroom the snake was gone, but drawers lay bottom-up on the floor and my can of talcum powder had been broken open. In Nannie's bath, the cosmetics had been invaded, and the dusting powder and bath salts spilled.

M. Guillaume's bouquet had been jerked from its vase and tossed haphazardly on the gilt-trimmed bureau. One pink rose lay on the floor forlornly, shedding petals. I took one look at it and started to cry.

"Tori, don't." C.D. took me in his arms and stroked my hair awkwardly.

I leaned into his comforting arms for just a moment, amazed at how good they felt. Then I straightened. "I'm all right. I just want to get my hands on the—the coyote who did this."

"Now you're talking." C.D. strode to the telephone.

I ran and grabbed it. "What do you think you're doing?"

"Calling the police, what do you think? The management's going to try to just hush this up if we don't take action."

"No." C.D. stared at me, and I added weakly, "We don't even know whether anything's been stolen."

"Okay, do you want to find that out first?" he asked. So room by room, we went through the suite. Nannie, ever organized, had brought an inventory list of suitcase contents, and my mother had seen to it that I had one, too.

Nothing was missing. "I thought so," C.D. commented. "If they'd found what they were looking for, they

57

wouldn't have trashed the place so thoroughly. They'd have stopped once they found it. Tori, think hard. What could they have been looking for?"

"I don't know," I said. "There's a rock star in the suite next door. Maybe somebody came to the wrong place, looking for money or even drugs or something."

"Somebody just happened to break in on you," C.D. said. "On top of what happened already? Tori, it's time we called the police."

By "what happened already" he meant the purse snatcher and the snake. *I* thought of Alvarez. And of Nannie's insistence that I stay with Monsieur Guillaume.

"No," I said, and it was as if Nannie's voice were speaking through me. "No, you don't understand."

"What's there to understand?" C.D. asked blankly.

"It all has to do with me."

He stared at me, and then he sat me down on the sitting room sofa, and I told him what I had figured out. Very carefully, so I wouldn't let slip anything about Hector Alvarez. Nannie was trusting me to keep out of that, and I couldn't let her down.

C.D. heard me through, and whistled. "Say you snapped a picture of something you shouldn't have. It didn't have to be of some native woman. With Argenteuil in town, there's probably lots going on that's not supposed to show up in the papers. Look what happened to me at the party."

"But I didn't see anything that looked strange."

"You're a tourist—*everything* in Morocco looks strange to you. That's why something top secret would have escaped your notice. But not your camera's." C.D.

frowned. "Wait a minute. Your film was stolen when your purse was snatched. So why these two break-ins today?"

"Because the film I'd shot wasn't in my purse. It was in the camera. And the snake could have been a—a warning."

"Tori, listen to me." I hadn't known I *wasn't* listening, but all at once C.D. was holding me, shaking me gently, his face very close to mine. "Tori, I know you're exhausted, but you've got to concentrate. *Where's your camera?* It wasn't here when we took inventory of the suite."

"That's because it's out in my pool locker," I murmured automatically. And then woke up fast. We stared at each other, and with one accord we both rose.

"It has to be there," I said. "There's only one key per locker, and the manager made a big deal about how we'd have to pay sixty dollars if we lost one, because they don't keep duplicates."

C.D. held out his hand. "Give me the key. I'll go get the camera."

"No way. I'm coming, too. I wouldn't stay here alone, anyway." I got the key ring, and, hand in hand, we strolled out to the pool terrace like lovers seeking privacy. C.D. stood with his arm around me, shielding me from view as I unlocked the locker. The handbag was there and the camera was inside. I grabbed the bag hastily, and we sauntered back inside as though we were in no hurry.

C.D. deadlocked the doors to the suite and pulled the curtains. "Is the film still there?" he asked. I nodded. My fingers trembled as I opened the back of the camera, and he had to take it from me and complete the job.

The film was safe.

"I can develop it myself tomorrow, if you want," C.D. said. "At the place that guy I know owns. But, Tori, if there's anything fishy in the pictures, you'll have to take them to the police. Or the American embassy, if that makes you feel better."

I shrugged. I'd cross that bridge when I came to it. Then C.D. looked at his watch. "It's almost tomorrow already! And neither of us ever got dinner. What if I call room service?"

We ordered dinner and ate in the suite's Moorish dining room. Then C.D. searched the suite again, thoroughly, checking locks on doors and windows, as I put things back in order as best I could. Then I went to bed in my bedroom, and C.D. bedded down on a sitting room sofa, right outside my door.

I never did call M. Guillaume.

7 I awoke to the strong smell of coffee and the clink of china. The sun was shining. I pulled on my robe and padded out to the sitting room, where C.D. was supervising a maid setting out breakfast in the little garden.

"You have time to take a shower if you make it fast," he said. "I borrowed your grandmother's shower; I hope she won't mind."

I took a fast shower and joined him in the garden, in both instances steeling myself against bad memories. "I called the hospital already," C.D. said. "I said I was Mrs. Clay's grandson. Hope you don't mind. She's doing fine, and you can see her after ten. While you do that, I'll develop your film. Okay?"

"Okay." C.D. was taking everything into his own hands. Back at home, I'd have resisted just out of principle, but so much had happened that I was glad for his help.

Nannie was out of intensive care and in her old spirits, meaning being a bad patient and insisting on getting out. "Not until afternoon," the doctor said firmly. He examined her arm, swollen and discolored from the snakebite, and looked at me. "Your grandmother was very, very lucky, mademoiselle. But she must—how do you say?—take it easy."

I wasn't ready to bet on her following the doctor's advice. "What happened last night, after I left?" she demanded when the doctor was gone.

The nurse was still there. I rolled my eyes in her direction and said glibly, "You know the book we've both been reading? I went on with it last night. When the heroine got back home, the—the man in green was gone. But somebody else had been there and trashed the place."

Nannie's eyes widened with alarm. "He didn't find what he was looking for," I said. "But the heroine thinks she's figured out what it was." She started, and I added hastily, "It's okay. She's perfectly safe."

"Guillaume?" Nannie asked.

I didn't want to go into that yet. "Don't worry, C.D.'s looking after me," I said. "I'll tell you the rest of the story when you get out of here this afternoon."

Nannie took my hand in her good one and looked at me fixedly. "Tori—"

I kissed her. "You take care, hear? C.D. and I will collect you right after lunch. Unless you want Monsieur Guillaume to do the honors?"

"No way," Nannie said forcibly.

C.D. was waiting for me in the hospital lobby. We went back to the hotel, and had lunch sent to the suite, and spread out the photographs to examine them. Not that it did any good. Even C.D., after going over them with a magnifying glass, conceded there was nothing that looked the least bit suspicious.

"All the same, somebody wanted them," he pointed out, returning them carefully to their folder. Then he frowned. "I still can't figure out how that snake fits in."

"Maybe it was a warning. Or an attempt to scare me out of the suite, so they could come back to trash it at their leisure."

"That makes sense." C.D. nodded respectfully.

"You have any problem getting the film developed?"

"Not really. The guy I know wasn't there. The place was shut up, like he'd taken off somewhere. When I saw him the day before yesterday, he said he might have to. He gave me a key to the place. Said he wanted me to have it in case I got a good picture and needed a darkroom fast."

"Like you did two days ago, you mean." But I was no longer as annoyed as I'd been back then. Too much else had happened.

The hotel manager phoned the room to inquire how Mme. Clay was doing. I said Mme. Clay was about to be discharged, and he insisted on sending a limousine to collect her. So C.D. and I rode to the hospital in it.

Nannie was weak, though she tried to pretend she was fine. We returned to the hotel and went back to the suite, and Nannie got rid of C.D. in the nicest possible way.

"Anything about Alvarez or my accident gotten out yet?" she demanded as soon as he was gone.

I shook my head. "Nothing in the papers about either. And it was no accident. And if you mean has Monsieur Guillaume found out, he hasn't, or he'd be here by now."

"So would your daddy, if he'd got wind of it," Nannie said wanly. "Give me the papers, Tori." She spread them out on one of the low tables. They were full of General Argenteuil's visit, but there was no coverage of Wednesday's private party.

The concierge buzzed our phone. The manager's compliments to Madame, and he would wait upon her later if she was up to it. Nannie said she'd see. A messenger had arrived from the American embassy, with an envelope for Mme. Clay, and M. Guillaume had phoned a number of times. "Have them send everything to the room," Nannie instructed me. "And tell them to hold all calls."

She was in an odd mood, very weak and remote but with her Irish up. When the envelope from the embassy came, she had me open it. It contained an invitation for us both to the ambassador's official party for General Argenteuil in Morocco's capital city, Rabat, next week. Nannie sat for several minutes staring into space after I'd read it aloud.

"It looks like you've acquired a new admirer," I teased.

Nannie started. "What?"

"General Argenteuil, who else? Why else would we have gotten a last-minute invitation?"

"Don't talk nonsense," Nannie said shortly, and closed her eyes.

I'd never seen her like this before, and it alarmed me. She just *sat* there, not even muttering about having to put her makeup on. Or about "all this precious travel time being wasted." I wondered whether she should have come home from the hospital so soon, after all. Or whether I should go over her head and phone M. Guillaume. Or Daddy.

But I also knew that I had no power to go over Nannie's head. Not even if she were at death's door. I was too much in awe of her. And I was scared stiff, not just of her, but of the danger I was in.

So I just sat there while Nannie spent most of the afternoon laboriously writing something with her left hand. Sat there, and surreptitiously pored over the photos C.D. had left with me. And then, abruptly, Nannie's voice broke through the little frozen shell surrounding me.

"Tori, help me change my clothes. We're going out."

"We're what? Nannie, you can't!"

"There's no such word as *can't* where I'm concerned," Nannie retorted. "Only *won't* or *too chicken*. Remember that. I'll be dang-blasted if I'm ready to let either of those apply to me. Now, come help me, Tori."

She'd made up her mind we were going out for dinner at that little Moroccan restaurant of hers. Without C.D. Wearing our Moroccan caftans. Nannie even, with her left hand, put on kohl eyeliner like the Moroccan women, and instructed me in arranging her hair in a new style to match. I'd never seen her before without her habitual braids.

I put on my new black caftan, and the red and gold tooled leather slippers, and a headscarf shot with silver, and had to admit they gave me a lift. We walked, slowly, out to the lobby. Nobody paid any attention to us. Near the front desk, Nannie halted. "Darling, go to the hotel gift shop and buy me a magazine I can read if the pain keeps me awake tonight, will you? In French or English. A fashion magazine will be fine, one of the slick ones."

I went and bought her a copy of *Elle*, and when I returned, Nannie was just emerging from the cubbyhole off the manager's office where guests could access their safe deposit boxes. She'd taken out a long gold chain and a pair of gold drop earrings and put them on, land knew how. There were no taxis out front, but the doorman insisted on summoning one of the hotel's private cars, so we rode to Nannie's little restaurant in style.

As soon as we were there, I was glad we'd come. It was in the new city, not far from the medina, and it was small and peaceful. From the grilled windows we had glimpses of the sea. A fountain splashed, and we sat on yellow-green leather poufs and ate fresh figs, and *b'stilla*— a kind of chicken pie—and orange slices sprinkled with rosewater.

The moon was out, silvering empty streets, when we emerged. There were no taxis to be seen. "We'll walk," Nannie said. I looked at her, and she repeated, "We'll walk. It isn't far. Hand me my magazine, Tori. I'll carry it."

I surrendered it dutifully.

So we walked for three blocks along the shoreline, and then inland. We walked slower and slower. I realized she was tiring. People passed us, but nobody looked at us. They must have thought we were both native women. We looked like them in the darkness.

We reached a corner that I recognized. "Only two blocks more," I turned to say to Nannie. And saw her sway.

"*Nan.*" I steered her quickly to a wall, and she leaned against it. Her face was drawn. "Nannie, I never should have let you talk me into this. Will you be okay if I leave you here? I'll run to the hotel and have them send a car."

"No," Nannie whispered. Her hands, both of them, were rolling the magazine convulsively. She wet her lips.

"No, darling," she said carefully. "We'll walk. Together. Just take my arm."

"Only if we go through the side street and through our garden," I said firmly. That was the closest way. Nannie hesitated, then she nodded. I took her good arm and steered her carefully.

We reached the next corner and started down the side street to our private garden. I tried not to think about the stranger there two nights before. We were safe now. Nobody'd know I was me. We looked like two native women.

It was somewhere in the middle of that last block I realized we were being followed. I could tell by the stiffening of Nannie's body that she knew it, too.

"Tori," Nannie whispered softer than breath. "Keep walking." We stepped down from the sidewalk into the street, and everything became slow motion. Like separate black-and-white pictures in a strip of film. Nannie and I crossing the street, and the streetlight showing no shadows but our own. There was the scent of tropical flowers; overpowering. Nannie and I stepping up on the opposite curb. The corner of our hotel coming into sight, maddeningly close.

And then a shadow, suddenly separating itself from ours. Looming behind us. Arms grabbing me. There was such a silence. I couldn't even scream. I saw light glint on something, a knife or a needle, coming at me as I struggled frantically.

Suddenly, my grandmother was in front of us. Suddenly, the rolled magazine was in her right hand. Her right arm was free of its sling and was shooting forward.

Nannie jabbed the point of the rolled magazine against my captor's neck. And there was still no sound. But he was slumping. I was free.

I twisted around and saw him fall to the street, blood gushing from his neck. From just the point where Nannie had felt for the pulse in Alvarez's throat.

"Nan, you *killed* him!" I whispered.

She had never looked like this, old and ill. But she grabbed my arm and forced me to start running, as she was running. We ran, stumbling and gasping, toward our garden entrance.

Just as we were almost to safe haven, headlights glared to life. An engine roared, heading toward us, gathering speed.

Nannie flung herself at me, spinning me out of the way onto the sidewalk. But she was hit. I saw her hit, saw her tossed in the air and left in a broken heap as the car roared away.

8   I lay there, stunned and aching. For a minute I could not breathe. Then breath returned, burning my lungs, and the image of what had happened seared my brain.

I pushed myself up, cautiously, on my hands, and forced myself to glance backward. Nannie lay on the street in a curious little heap. I wouldn't have known it was human if I hadn't seen what had happened.

I didn't know if it was still alive.

I wanted to run to her, but I didn't dare. The car that had run us down might be lurking somewhere, around a corner from this deserted street. The man who had tried to abduct me might have a backup hiding somewhere.

The man who had tried to abduct me—the man who lay out there, dead. I couldn't see him from here. He was back around the corner. But Nannie was here.

I kept down on the ground, and I crawled to her. Close up, she looked like an old native woman. Her dark blue caftan was a dim blur. She lay on her right side, on the arm still swollen from snakebite, the arm that nonetheless had killed to save my life. The silver-shot veil that covered her head had fallen back, and a wisp of white hair showed, not dramatic now but poignant. Her eyes were closed, but I thought I saw a pulse flutter in her temple.

I leaned close to her ear and whispered, *"Nannie."*

Her eyelids moved. Thank God. Her eyes looked straight at me with an urgent question.

"The car's gone. We're alone."

Her voice was so faint I had to lean close to hear. "Thank God . . . Tori, stay down."

"I know. But I've got to go for help. Is it okay to leave you?"

"No," Nannie said, and she didn't mean she wouldn't be all right, she meant I mustn't go. The fingers of her left hand groped, and I put mine into them, and she clutched them tightly. Then, muscle by muscle, she flexed her left arm, her left leg. The caftan stirred as she tested her torso, too. She gasped, and I saw her lips flatten with pain. Then, very carefully, the toes of her right foot stirred . . . the muscle in her instep . . . in her right calf. Another gasp escaped her, and she stopped.

"Tori . . . turn me over. On my stomach."

"Nannie, *no!*"

"Yes. Mustn't—be found here. *Now.* Carefully."

Maybe it was because she could dominate me, maybe because I knew she was right, but I did it. Slowly. Carefully. Nannie groaned with pain; her right leg looked all twisted and I realized sickly something must be broken. But inch by inch, pulling herself with her outstretched left arm, Nannie dragged herself up out of the gutter. Onto the sidewalk. Down the few interminable feet to our own garden gate, as I crawled with her. I got the gate unlocked and open, and eased her in, trying not to touch her right arm or leg. I slammed the gate shut and locked it from the inside, then knelt beside her.

"Nannie, can you hear me? I'm going for help.

Through the hotel. You'll be all right here."

Nannie's eyelids, rather than her head, nodded. She was weakening fast. But as I tried to rise, her left hand grabbed my caftan with surprising strength. Her eyes opened wide and burned into mine. *"Don't tell . . ."* The eyelids closed.

Don't tell what? About the man in the street, I sure as shooting wouldn't. He was around the corner, and somebody else could find him. I had the murder weapon still tucked mechanically beneath my arm. A fashion magazine—who would believe that, anyway? But there was no way I could avoid telling that Nannie'd been struck down by a car.

All this rushed through my head as I unlocked the door into the suite, raced through it, dumping the magazine in the trash on the way, and out into the corridor. Maybe running around the outside of the hotel would have been faster, and maybe somebody was waiting to grab me if I did. I ran to the front desk, and it was as if a whole unbelievable scene were being repeated, except that this time I was fully clothed. The hotel people, running to help. A small spellbound group of onlookers. An ambulance siren. This time I rode to the hospital in the ambulance.

Nannie had been unconscious in the garden when we'd reached her, but by the time we got to the hospital she was struggling out of the mists and in great pain. They wouldn't let me into the emergency room with her, and this time I waited alone.

At last a dark-skinned, worried doctor came to me. "Mademoiselle, you are with the hit-and-run victim?"

"Yes. She's my grandmother. How is she?"

"Her hip is broken, and her leg also. We must anesthetize her to set the bones, but she won't allow us to sedate her. Also, we have no medical history on her or identification."

I said loudly, "She's Mrs. Henry McCausland Clay. My grandfather was head of McCausland Industries." Now if ever was the time to exploit the family name. One of Granddaddy's "industries" was McCausland Pharmaceuticals, and I was gambling the doctor had heard of it. He had. "Also, she was here overnight last night. For snakebite. There must be some record. I can fill in the rest. First let me see her."

"For a few minutes only. You must convince her, mademoiselle, to allow us to proceed with treatment."

They took me to her. The emergency room didn't look that different from emergency rooms back home. Nannie, racked with pain, lay so very still, surrounded by IV tubes. Her eyes pleaded, and her parched lips struggled to form words.

"I understand," I said reassuringly. "Don't talk." I was making a covenant of silence about the killing, but the hospital staff would think I was telling *her* not to talk. "Nannie, they have to sedate you. They have to set bones. I'll take care of everything. I swear."

Her eyelids closed and she nodded. A nurse touched my arm and led me out.

It wasn't me, it was some zombie with my name and face who sat with the nurse and answered questions obediently. Nannie's name, address (home and local), age. Medical history, as far as I knew it. Name of her doctor in the States, if needed—thank goodness I remembered that, because I'd once fallen off my bike while visiting her. My voice said, "I think she brought medical information with her. It's probably with her passport. I can get it."

"I doubt that will be necessary until morning." That was the doctor, reappearing. "Your grandmother is in the operating theater now. Thanks to providence, one of the country's best orthopedic men was available. It will be some hours before the bone reconstruction is completed, mademoiselle, and more hours before she will be conscious. I think it would be wise for you to get some sleep."

"I want to stay here."

"It would be wise," he repeated, "for you to return to your hotel. Is there someone who can be summoned to be with you? You must not be alone."

That's true for reasons you don't know, I thought hysterically. Monsieur Guillaume and his wife would be there in an instant if I called them, and they would take over. But there were things I could not let them take over. Things I had to do. I came to a decision.

"I have a friend I can call," I said. "If you'll please show me to a phone."

The kind nurse had reappeared. "I will show you, mademoiselle," she said gently. "Mademoiselle, I have here Madame's jewelry. We had to remove it before she went into surgery. If you will look at it, and sign a receipt."

She spread it out on the table. Nannie's wedding and engagement rings, and the diamond eternity ring Granddaddy had given her one anniversary. Her watch. The earrings and chain she'd gotten out of the safe deposit box to wear to dinner. I nodded dully, signed a receipt, and put them into my purse. She led me to a phone.

Providence, as the doctor would say, be thanked that I remembered the cheap hotel C.D. was staying at. Providence be thanked that the night clerk produced C.D.

"Nannie's in the hospital again," I said briefly. "The same one. Will you come get me?"

"Soon as I get my clothes on," C.D. said, and was as good as his word.

We didn't talk at the hospital. C.D. seemed to know it wouldn't be a good idea. He collected me, and gave the hospital the phone number of my hotel, and herded me into a taxi. "Hotel Grande," he ordered.

I wet my lips. "No. Wait. I want to go the long way round." I gave directions for the route through the side street where I'd been grabbed. C.D. looked at me closely, but nodded to the driver.

We rode in silence, C.D. holding tight to both my hands. I knew he could feel me stiffen as we turned into the street, but he asked no questions. I stared out the window.

There was no body in the street. It had vanished, just as Hector Alvarez had vanished.

The cab pulled up at the entrance to the hotel. C.D. helped me out and paid the driver. He walked me like a windup doll down the corridor and steered me into the suite. After double-locking the door behind us, he came over to put his arms around me. "Tori, I know you're in shock, but can you tell me what happened?"

"Not now."

"She was hit by a car on the street outside, I know that much. The night manager talked to me as we came in. Just tell me, does it have anything to do with what happened yesterday?"

"I said not now."

C.D. looked at me hard, but let me be, except for ordering tea. When it came he sat with me and made me drink it. I wished he'd leave me alone. I knew without our discussing it that he'd stay the night, and I was grateful, but I wished he'd give me space.

In shock. Yes, I was in shock. I'd been in Morocco three days—it must be the fourth day by now, well after midnight. In that time a man had died, hammering to get through our garden door. I'd been mugged. Somebody'd planted a poisonous snake in my bathroom drawer. Our rooms had been trashed. Somebody'd tried to abduct or kill me. And my grandmother had killed a man, and had nearly been killed herself.

My grandmother was the most civilized, most totally *herself* person that I knew. I could have sworn I knew her through and through. Yet in those three days she'd turned into a total stranger who could move a body and not bat an eye, who could kill by instinct—with just a *magazine*.

Shock.

I got up and went to Nannie's bedroom, clutching her jewelry in my hands. I ought to put it into her safe deposit box, I knew. Or in one of my own, if there was no way to get into hers. That key must be in her purse, which I'd brought back from the hospital. But I couldn't force myself to walk out to the front desk right then.

Nannie's suitcases sat on the ledge provided. I had a key for them, because at her insistence we'd exchanged duplicate luggage keys ("Never know when you may lose one," Nannie had said). Mechanically, I got my purse, got the key, opened up her overnight case, and dropped the jewelry in. It landed on the open box of writing paper she'd been using just before we went to dinner, and I left it there. I could picture her as I locked the case—Nannie, sitting all afternoon in the filtered light from the garden, writing some long letter. I'd seen her put the letter on top of the writing paper when she put it away. I blotted out the image, and went to my own room, and to bed.

Just as I was falling asleep a faint realization stirred. That letter wasn't on top of the writing paper anymore.

9 When I woke up Saturday morning, I felt as if I'd been up for days without sleep, which was too darn close to truth. And I felt as if I were coming down with the flu, which had better not be true. I was being very careful about not eating any unpeeled fruits or vegetables, and about drinking bottled water. But my insides still felt as if they'd been mauled in a cement mixer.

My body ached, too, from the way Nannie'd slammed me onto the sidewalk, but that didn't matter. She'd saved my life. And she'd killed to do it. And there I was, face-to-face with *that* again. Each time something happened this week, I thought grimly, it was worse than the time before.

There had been no dead body in the street when we came home. No account of a dead body in the paper. Still nothing in print about Hector Alvarez, his death, or his burial. And the hotel management, who were falling all over themselves about Mme. Henry McCausland Clay's welfare, had never mentioned the matter of Hector Alvarez at all.

I felt like I'd stepped into a Hitchcock movie—or, I thought, into *Casablanca*. I'd seen *Casablanca* on TV a couple of times, and wept buckets, but I hadn't expected Morocco today to be like that.

Early Saturday morning I received a phone call from

the hospital. Mme. Clay required another operation, and wouldn't permit it till she'd first spoken to Mademoiselle. I went to the hospital alone, though I had to practically hog-tie C.D. to get away.

Nannie was nearly unrecognizable, all but her eyes, for she was locked into a system of traction and IV bottles and machines. A nurse hovered, after warning me not to tire her. "Madame is heavily sedated, and drifting in and out of consciousness."

Nannie's words, when I leaned close enough to hear her whisper, were definitely lucid. "Guillaume—see him *now*," she whispered.

I nodded. "Don't worry. I'll take care of everything."

Nannie's head shook, ever so faintly. "He must . . . send you home . . . plane—*today*."

I straightened, frowning, and Nannie's fingers tried to reach for mine. The nurse hurried over. "Mademoiselle, you must *not* upset her." So I nodded vaguely, indicating a promise I did not intend to keep. Nannie relaxed slightly, and her eyes closed. The nurse checked her pulse. "Mademoiselle, it is time for you to go."

I started to turn away, and then something stopped me. Maybe it was because Nannie and I were so close, no matter what. The nurse was busy now at the machines, and didn't see, but I did. Nannie gave a faint, almost imperceptible cry, and her head turned back and forth in weak desperation. Her lips were forming syllables that I bent close to see.

"... *Fat man . . . must find—fat man . . .*"

She's delirious, I thought dully. I heard authoritative footsteps behind me—a doctor, arriving. The nurse hurried forward with a hypodermic. "We must begin anesthesia, mademoiselle," she murmured, reaching for Nannie's arm.

Just as she did so, Nannie's eyes opened and looked straight into mine. Calling me, urgently—

In spite of the nurse and doctor, I leaned down, my ear to Nannie's lips. I could barely hear the faint sounds she gasped out before she fell unconscious. *"O.S.S. . . . "*

O.S.S.? It made no sense at all.

I left the hospital and headed out into the street, a modern street of a perfectly modern city. It all seemed so familiar till I saw the palm trees, the veiled women, and men in fezzes or turbans, and the beggars. In the bright sunlight, it looked so unthreatening.

And yet I was in danger. And Nannie's life, right now, lay in the balance. And I did not know why. I stood there among the ring of outstretched hands, and I was sure of nothing except that both of us had been caught up in something terribly dangerous. That Nannie had killed someone who was after me, for reasons yet unknown.

Maybe Hector Alvarez was murdered, too. The thought struck me out of nowhere. *And Nannie had recognized him.* I could not forget the way she had frozen, staring down. It was crazy, it didn't make sense, because I'd been with Nannie every minute since we'd been in Morocco, and when else could she have met him? *Forty-five years ago,* my crazy thoughts answered me.

Had Nannie also recognized the man attacking me last night? I didn't want to think that, but I couldn't help it. If it were true, there was a whole world of facts that Nannie was keeping from me. *But she'd never have brought me here if she'd thought I'd be in danger,* my mind protested childishly.

Would she?

The only thing more terrible than these things I was thinking was the idea of Nannie's killing that man last night being found out. Nannie charged with murder in a third-world country. No matter that she'd been defending me; we had no witness. I'd seen movies. I'd seen how frantic Nannie had been at the idea of my getting mixed up with a police investigation here.

I came to, to find myself standing motionless and blocking the sidewalk. I couldn't just stand there. I had to do something. What? I started walking, and presently found myself where I'd been with Nannie a day or so earlier, the better-class shopping area in the new city, near the shore. I walked and walked, past the brass shops and the caftan shops and jewelry stores, and a stranger with my face stared back at me from the reflecting windows.

10 And then a voice, a familiar, comfortable American voice, said, "Tori! For goodness' sake!" It was Mr. Entwhistle from our table on the cruise ship.

He stood there looking so matter-of-fact and reassuring that I could have cried. "Mrs. Entwhistle's out shopping with a lady she met," he said, "so I'm doing some wandering on my own. Is your grandmother around? Maybe we can all meet somewhere later." He peered at me closely. "Why, Tori! What's the matter, my dear? Is something wrong?"

"It's Nannie," I said. "She's in the hospital." Then I did break down, not crying but bending double to gasp for breath. I started shaking.

Mr. Entwhistle reacted exactly as my grandfather would have. Within minutes he had me sitting at a table in a secluded part of a hotel lobby, and coffee and pastries ordered. "These things are a lot sweeter than I usually like," he said, passing me the baklava, "but they grow on you. Can you drink this Moorish coffee? It's like mud to me, but I've found it hopeless trying to get anything else."

The coffee, thick and sweet and boiled to a foam with milk, was like syrup, but I choked it down. I could do with a jolt of caffeine. Mr. Entwhistle sat with massive calm while I sipped it. I set the little cup in its saucer and took an experimental breath. "I'm all right now. I think."

"Now tell me about your grandmother," he said.

So I did, carefully, omitting everything between when we'd left the restaurant and when the car had loomed. I gave the impression the whole thing had been an accident, and I don't think he suspected anything. He had enough to digest as it was. Mr. Entwhistle offered to phone the American consulate and check out the doctors taking care of Nannie, and I accepted gratefully. He left me sitting in the lobby while he did so. I was in full view of the doorman and the bell captain's staff, so I thought I was safe enough.

When Mr. Entwhistle returned, he was smiling. "It's an excellent hospital, and what you were told was true: that orthopedist has an international reputation. He trained in New York. Here's a name and number to call at the consulate if you need further help. How are you going to manage, Tori? From the sound of it, your grandmother will be in the hospital for some time, and you shouldn't be here alone."

"I'm not alone. C.D.'s here, you remember him. And there's the manager of the Tangier office of McCausland Industries." I stopped blankly. "Monsieur Guillaume. I was supposed to call him." It was finally time, I decided, to do what Nannie had asked me—though I had no intention of following her second request, to leave her in Morocco alone and helpless while I flew home.

"I can do that for you." With calm efficiency Mr. Entwhistle got all the particulars about Nannie from me, and excused himself again. He was gone longer this time. It dawned on me that this was Saturday, and Monsieur

Guillaume was unlikely to be at his office. But Mr. Entwhistle wasn't a retired military officer for nothing. He came back briskly.

"Guillaume sounds like a responsible chap. He's going to lean on the hospital to make sure Nancy gets the best of care. He'll take care of finances and all that, too. I told him not to phone your family; I figured you'd prefer to do that yourself. He offered to send his wife here to be with you, and to have you come stay with them, but I told him I was looking after you for the moment."

"Thanks." Mme. Guillaume was kind, but she reminded me too much of some of Mother's socialite friends. I drank some more coffee, and its warmth started penetrating the chill inside me. "What are you and Mrs. Entwhistle doing here, anyway? I thought you were going on with the ship to Gibraltar."

"We did. And frankly, within twenty-four hours we got bored. So I convinced my wife we'd have more fun if we flew over here. We'll stay a short while, then take a plane to meet the cruise again in Italy. This is the hotel we're staying in, by the way. You can call us anytime you need us."

"I appreciate that," I said, and meant it. But there were too many secrets I had to guard for me to throw myself into Mrs. Entwhistle's motherly arms. Something stirred in my memory. "Mr. Entwhistle, you met Nannie once back when she was here during the war. What do you remember about her then? Or what did she tell you?"

"I didn't know her *here*," he corrected me. "It was in England, where I was stationed. She was sent there after she left here." He smiled, remembering. "She was pretty mysterious, even as a girl." *But she hasn't been, not till now*, something in me wanted to cry out, but I held it in. "Why, she didn't even let on about that prize-winning war photograph she took. To hear her, she was strictly into fashion and society. Even your grandfather heard about it from someone else. I'll bet there are a lot of good stories she could tell."

I wet my lips. "Did you ever hear of anything called O.S.S.?" I asked casually. "I think maybe it has something to do with World War Two."

"'Maybe it has something to do with'?" Mr. Entwhistle looked amused—and relieved at imagining I was getting my mind off Nannie. "What are they teaching in history classes these days, young lady?"

"Then it does mean something."

"Only Office of Strategic Services. Which just happened to be the World War Two forerunner of the C.I.A. In other words, the U.S. spy network, and from what I remember, it was pretty active here in Morocco, and in Spain, and other neutral countries." He slapped his hand down on the table. "What made you ask about O.S.S.?"

"I heard about it somewhere," I said vaguely. Pieces were falling into place, forming a disturbing picture. Nance O'Neill here, during the war. Nance O'Neill with her camera.

I picked up my big tote bag, which I was using in place of my slashed handbag. "Mr. Entwhistle, I think I'd better be getting back to our hotel. There might be word from the doctors, or from Monsieur Guillaume."

Mr. Entwhistle paid for our snack and insisted on escorting me door-to-door, for which I was more relieved than I could say. C.D. was still in the suite, pacing back and forth and furious with worry.

"Do you know how long you've been gone? I was beginning to wonder if you'd been kidnapped!"

"*Don't say that.*"

"Okay, I won't. Calm down." C.D. looked at me closely, then came over and brushed back my hair. "Don't be so afraid, kid. Nance O'Neill's a fighter. And so are you." He gave me a brotherly kiss on the top of my head and said, with unexpected perception, "You need to be alone. I'm going out for a while to scrounge around. I'll be back later."

"Wait." I went to Nannie's purse, took out her keys to the suite and garden, and gave them to him. He nodded. Then he went.

I called the hospital. Nannie was out of surgery and doing well but heavily sedated. Monsieur Guillaume had ordered round-the-clock private nurses, English-speaking ones. The front desk said Monsieur Guillaume had called me, twice. I told them to hold all calls except from the hospital.

I paced around the suite, trying not to think because I knew pieces fell into place faster if I didn't force them. The trash had been emptied and the magazine was gone with it, I realized; I only hoped the maid hadn't noticed any bloodstains.

I tried to decide what to do about notifying Dad, and decided to let that ride, too. He'd either fly over, make me go home, or both, and I had a gut-wrenching instinct both things would be wrong.

I'd write him a letter. I'd have it ready to send, with all

tellable details, and Monsieur Guillaume would get it sent by overnight mail when necessary. The suite was amply provided with stationery, but I went to Nannie's suitcase to use hers instead, to give my courage a boost.

Nannie's jewelry, including her diamond rings, lay winking quietly at me atop the stationery box, and they made me cry.

I ought to put them in the safe deposit box, I knew. Methodically, I got Nannie's purse again and put it and the jewelry into my own big tote bag.

I went to the front desk, prepared to raise a big stink about getting access to Nannie's box. To my surprise, since I had the key, I had no fight. The manager personally escorted me into the private cubicle, murmured sympathy and concern for Nannie, and after using his key on the box left me with it to use ours.

I waited till he was gone to do so, and was I glad I had.

The first thing I saw when I lifted the lid was a fat envelope of Nannie's favorite pale gray stationery. It must be the letter she'd been writing yesterday, I thought; she must have stashed it when she got her jewelry, while she'd sent me for that magazine. The envelope was addressed to me.

I lifted it, and then my heart froze as my fingers froze.

Underneath the envelope lay a gun. A familiar gun, black and silver, the silver part elaborately monogrammed. *H. McC. C.* It was Granddaddy's gun. I ought to know, because he'd taught me to shoot, just like he'd taught my father. Taught me target shooting and skeet shooting. I kind of liked shooting at those clay disks with a rifle, calculating to allow for projectile time and the amount of the gun's recoil. But I was really kind of scared of the guns themselves. Especially handguns.

Nannie hated guns, all guns. She wouldn't touch them, she'd hated Granddaddy teaching me. But she'd brought Granddaddy's prized pistol with her to Morocco, and she hadn't told me.

And the gun was loaded.

11 Like a sleepwalker I took the gun, and put it and the letter into my bag. I put Nannie's jewelry in the box, and shut and locked it, and rang the bell to call the manager. We exchanged polite remarks. I went back to the suite, feeling as though snakes were slithering around my stomach.

I took a shower; I needed the hot water pounding on me. While I showered I realized that *one* thing about the gun, at least, made sense. Nannie could never have gotten it through an airline security check, but she'd insisted on taking the train to New York to meet me at the start of the cruise. Now I knew why. And I'd seen the way she'd gotten herself waved through ship customs, with her usual charm. . . .

In the terry robe the hotel provided, I sat down in a patch of sunlight to read Nannie's letter. It was afternoon now, and I'd had no lunch, but I couldn't eat. I slit the envelope carefully. Nannie had written her name across the seal, as if making sure I'd know if it were tampered with. I unfolded the letter and flattened it carefully. So many pages, closely written on both sides and so laboriously, with her left hand.

My very dear Victoria —

That's the way she always wrote to me when she was being serious. My eyes stung as I read, and as I read I was swept back through time. For the first time she was letting me see her, not as my grandmother, but as Nance O'Neill.

Nance O'Neill, who had a streak of wild Irish in her, who graduated from high school at sixteen and, instead of the college she could not afford, took her high-school journalism experience, supplemented with skills learned in an after-school job with Kodak, and talked her way into an editorial assistant job with a fashion magazine.

> ... Pop could have killed me, because it meant commuting to New York. But he let me do it—probably because he knew he couldn't stop me. After a year and a half, I blarneyed my way into being sent as a photographer's assistant to cover the European couture collections. I was in Spain when World War II broke out, and I simply stayed. Spain was neutral, and I kept telling the family I was safe.
>
> Dear heart, this is something that's hard to write, because even your grandfather never knew. I fell in love with a British soldier attached to the British embassy in Madrid—I'll call him Paul—and when he was sent to North Africa in 1940 on a secret mission, I managed to get the magazine to send me there, too.
>
> While I was there, I was recruited by an American officer Paul knew to be a secret agent of the O.S.S. . . .

I put down the letter and closed my eyes and made myself breathe deeply. This *was* like something out of *Casablanca*. I could see the title credits for a B-grade movie: *Grandma Was a Spy*.

All these years Nannie, the only totally honest person that I knew, had lived a lie, or at least a secret life. Nannie, who despised being two-faced as much as I did—or had led me to believe that—had kept it secret even from me. The closeness, the bond of "knowing and being known" between us that I'd valued so, had all been a lie.

I forced myself to read on.

> My cover was to be photographer and gossip columnist for the fashion magazine. My real assignment was to get photographs of nationals of Allied or neutral nations who had contacts in Morocco with known Nazis. The U.S. government needed to know who was secretly collaborating.

She'd even been flown back to the horse country of Virginia for training in the whole arsenal of secret agent skills. Including how to cut a jugular vein with a rolled magazine? I thought. And how to get away with it?

Why was she telling me this now? There could be just one reason. Because of what had happened. Because she was afraid she was marked for death for some reason, and knew it was necessary for me to have the facts.

I read on, half-fascinated, half-repelled. All of a sudden, and at last, I was seeing the real Nance O'Neill.

She had been only a couple of years older than I, alone on a continent at war. In love with a British soldier, and working with members of the French Resistance on behalf of the O.S.S.

> I never figured on falling in love a second time. He was a French resistance officer. I knew him only by his code name, Jaguar. His hair was blue-black, and his eyes were, too. His spirit was as wild and reckless as my own. He was a total monarchist, burning with a vision of bringing

France back to its former glory. Time goes all out of joint in times of crisis. Within a few weeks he and Paul and I were locked into a painful triangle.

And, I read, into a dangerous game of espionage that flowed across Morocco and Algiers and into Spain. And then—something happened.

On a mission Nance O'Neill was supposed to be a part of, but reached too late for a reason she did not explain, Paul was killed. Killed, with two members of the French Resistance, by a bomb thrown into the cave where they were hiding.

I stopped reading, my eyes full of tears. A fist seemed to have closed around my heart. Oh, Nan, I thought. No wonder she understood so much so well. I opened my eyes and kept on reading through the blur.

They'd been carrying important information. And the only way the Nazis could have known was if, as Paul had suspected, we had a mole—a double agent—in our midst.

I was in Casablanca when I heard, drinking coffee in a café. People were getting drunk, laughing, singing, and I couldn't bear it. I ran to the Jaguar. I knew where he lived. It was the middle of the night, and dangerous for me to be on the streets, but I ran there. He wasn't home. I knocked and knocked, like the man at our garden door on Wednesday night. And because I was afraid, when he still didn't answer I pulled out my hatpin and picked the lock. I let myself in.

The Jaguar had gone out in such haste that an oil lamp still burned on his table, and the book he'd been writing in was still open on the table. I knew what it must be. It was his private diary, and it was in code—

As I'd read, the afternoon sunlight had been fading. Suddenly, it was much darker. A shadow loomed over me from behind, cutting off the garden's light.

I acted on instinct. My hands grasped the gun lying in my lap, the gun I already knew was loaded, and my thumb flicked off the safety catch. I swung round, pointing the gun straight at the garden doors.

12 All at once the scene dissolved into comedy. The late sunlight glinted on a crest of bright red hair, and C.D.'s shocked voice shouted, "Tori, don't shoot!"

I jammed the gun and the letter into the pocket of my robe and ran to the garden doors. My hands were all thumbs fumbling with the safety latch. At last I got it open, and C.D. slid in quickly.

"What did you think you were doing?" he demanded. "And where on earth did you get a gun?"

"It's all right, it's my grandfather's," I said idiotically.

"For pete's sake, put it away! It could be loaded."

"It is," I said giddily. The look on his face made me start to laugh. I laughed and laughed, till I was bent double, hugging my sides. And then the tears were running down my face, and I was shaking uncontrollably.

C.D. led me to a sofa. He got the gun from my pocket and laid it gingerly on a chair. Not the letter; even in the state I was in, I noticed that he didn't take the letter. I started sobbing, and C.D. put his arms around me from behind and hugged me tight, rocking with me. I couldn't stop shaking.

"I feel so ashamed," I gulped.

"Don't. You've had some terrible shocks. No wonder you're all shook up."

You don't know the half of it, I thought. I started laughing again, and C.D., alarmed, shifted his seat to face me. "Oh, Lord, Tori, don't start that again! Something else has happened, hasn't it? No, don't turn away. Wipe your eyes, and try to tell me." He pressed a handkerchief into my hand.

"I wish I could tell you," I said when I could speak. "You don't know how much I wish I could. But it's not my right to tell."

"Is it your grandmother's?" C.D. said at once. I must have flinched. "Does it have anything to do with those papers in your pocket?"

I'd had no experience with lying. "Please don't ask me," I said thickly.

"Okay," C.D. said at last. "I'll go at it another way. Ever since you got to Morocco you've been jittery—"

"Haven't I had enough to make me jittery? The snake, this room that night—" I stopped because C.D.'s head was shaking firmly.

"That's what I thought at first, but it started before that. You were like that the first afternoon I called, and I don't think it was just because of my cheap shot with that photograph, or my big mouth on the ship the night before." He broke off, staring at me. "Come to think of it, your *grandmother* was shook on the ship that night. Not just angry with me for blowing her cover. It was more than that."

"Stop it, please!"

C.D. got up and started walking. "Somebody tried to steal your purse. We thought it was on account of that film, but neither of us found anything incriminating on it.

Somebody planted a snake in here. Somebody trashed the place. And then Nance O'Neill got run down by a hit-and-run driver in a deserted street. Have I missed anything? Tori, *look* at me! Maybe we were wrong, maybe you weren't the target. Maybe it was Nance O'Neill they've been after all along! *Why?* Because I blurted out to all the world who she really was?"

"Stop it!"

C.D. froze. "That's it, isn't it? There may be something in those pictures we don't see, maybe not, but it's *Nance O'Neill* who's the real threat. Tori, you've got to tell me. Or better yet, the police. Don't you know by now you're in something way over your head, and you can't protect your grandmother all alone?" He strode to the nearest phone.

"No!" I flung myself at him and wrenched it away.

"Then tell me." C.D.'s eyes narrowed. "There's something in those papers, isn't there? That's why you're like this."

He reached for me, and I shouted *"No!"* again and blundered off into a wall. I was hyperventilating, and I couldn't stop. C.D. took my hands and helped me get control. He put his arms around me again, but he didn't reach toward that pocket. For the rest of my days I'll bless him for that. He didn't try to take the letter.

"You don't know how much I wish I could tell you all of it," I whispered. "But I can't. I don't even know it all."

"Okay, we'll let it go at that. Just so you know, when and if you can, I'm here. By the way," he said gently, "I'm not a total clown. Or a total blabbermouth. I can be trusted with secrets if I know they're secrets. There's a lot of stuff you don't know about me. Like that I'm an army brat from two generations, and my dad was a Green Beret and was killed in Nam. And one of the things this trip's for is to photograph Allied battlefields from World War Two. If you don't believe any of that, you can check it out. I can be serious when I have to be."

Somehow knowing all that, and the World War II connection, made me breathe easier. And I couldn't keep all my secrets to myself. It wasn't safe. If anything happened to me, who would look after Nannie? But it was more than that. I trusted C.D.

"I can tell you this much," I said at last. "Something more did happen. I found out Nannie's being a photographer here during the war was just a cover. She was an agent of the O.S.S."

C.D. whistled. Unlike me, he knew at once what those letters stood for. "So somebody *could* be gunning for her. How did you find out?"

"She left a letter for me, in her safe deposit box with Granddaddy's gun. And this morning—"

"Then *she* thinks somebody's after her. No wonder she was so mad at me. But why, after all these years—I thought all World War Two secrets were out of the can by now." C.D. stopped. "What were you going to say about this morning?"

"Just that that's when she told me. At the hospital. They were getting her doped up for surgery, and she was frantic to tell me something. She whispered 'O.S.S.,' but I didn't know what she meant. Not till I found her letter. I thought she was just delirious. It didn't make sense any more than the stuff she said about finding a fat man."

"What?" C.D. asked me, very quietly.

"Finding a fat man—*oh!*" The thought struck me so suddenly that the words escaped me before I could hold them back. "Maybe she meant the man who died in the garden!"

C.D. started. Then he put me in a chair, pulled another up to face me, and took my hands. "Tori, you've gone too far to stop. What man in the garden? When?"

I'd gone so far that if I left him to fill in the blanks for himself, it could be worse than telling him the truth. I just thanked God I hadn't let slip about the second corpse. So I told him. Carefully. C.D. heard me all the way through, prompting me occasionally with brief questions.

"No wonder," he said at last, deep in thought. And then, "Tori, I think I have it. She didn't mean a fat man, she meant *the* Fatman. That's the nickname his old war buddies have for Max. My photo gallery friend I told you about, remember? He's a big tub of lard, and he's around your grandmother's age. And I know for a fact he was in these parts during World War Two."

We stared at each other. I wet my lips. "Did—did he see the picture you took of Nannie?"

C.D. nodded. "I was burbling on about the thrill of meeting Nance O'Neill, and he didn't say a word. Which, now that I think of it, was out of character." He pushed me toward my bedroom. "Get some clothes on. We'd better talk to Max. Maybe your grandmother was sending you to him. And maybe he was sending this Alvarez to her."

We careened off in a taxi, after I'd dressed and put the gun and the letter back in the safe deposit box. I emptied the contents from Nannie's big briefcase-like handbag, filled it with what I needed, and took it with me.

"I don't know when I'll get time to buy another handbag," I told C.D. in the cab, trying to make light conversation for the benefit of the driver. "Speaking of which, remind me to buy toothpaste while we're out. I left ours on the ship. If Nannie gets back and finds I'm still using her baking soda . . ." It was better to think of Nannie's return than to think how long her recovery could take.

The taxi squealed to a stop. "Hey, we're not there yet," C.D. protested. The driver, in a stream of Arabic and French, pointed and gesticulated. I looked, and something lurched within me. We were back at the corner of the street where I'd been mugged, where C.D.'d charged to my rescue.

"He's trying to tell us the street's closed for some reason," C.D. said. "Probably because of all the peddlers. That's Max's place, there with the blinds down." And then, in a totally different voice, "Uh-oh."

He was staring, with narrowed eyes, at the exact building in front of which I'd photographed the little beggar with the irresistible eyes. The shop that had been closed.

It was closed now, but with a difference. Police barricades—different from those back home, but recognizable nonetheless—were up, and policemen, recognizable in and out of uniform, were everywhere.

I pushed some money toward the driver, got out of the cab, and ran forward with C.D. close behind. And then I saw the detective who had interrogated us at the hotel, and I dropped back. "You find out," I hissed to C.D., and he gave me one shrewd glance and raced ahead. Somewhere between the cab and here, his *Washington Post* press pass and his camera had become prominent. I tried to fade unnoticed into the crowd, and waited. But my eyes were busy.

There was an ambulance, along with police cars, in the narrow street. Pretty soon the ambulance attendants came out of the shop door, carrying a stretcher. A totally covered stretcher. The police followed it, and so did C.D., but even before C.D. came loping over, I knew.

He steered me off to a nearby coffeehouse and succeeded in getting me fruit juice instead of coffee.

"He's dead, isn't he?" I said.

C.D. nodded. "Same scenario as your place the night you came." That meant dead of a sudden heart attack, no sign of violence. We stared at each other.

"And," C.D. said carefully, "the same scene decor as your place the *second* night."

The picture sprang vividly before my eyes, as clearly as if I'd seen it. Premises totally trashed . . . papers mussed and crumpled, photographs torn down . . . and whatever was being sought, not found. And a fat man, C.D.'s friend the Fatman, lying dead among the ruins.

13 "When did he die?" I asked in a matter-of-fact voice, and C.D. answered in the same way.

"It must have been hours ago." And then, harshly, "The rigor'd worn off, and the body'd started to—in this heat—" He swallowed hard. "God . . . he was such a nice old guy, it isn't fair!"

"I know," I said. "I know."

"It may have been right after I was here to develop that film. I could have been there when—"

"Don't even think about it."

"Why not?" He looked straight at me. "I don't believe it was a heart attack."

"I don't, either. Too much coincidence. But the police said the—the first one was definitely that."

"Just like the hit-and-run was definitely an accident? Not to mention the snake? You can forget about keeping me out of any of this from now on," C.D. said bluntly. "I'm in all the way. As if I hadn't been already."

"What happened while you were in there?" I asked. C.D. shrugged.

"I didn't get to take any pictures, but I remember everything I saw. I just did my eager-beaver American photographer routine, and the police tossed a few bones to me and then threw me out. If they're suspicious, they sure weren't showing it." C.D. had ordered himself coffee, and he bolted it down. "Know what I think, the police aren't going to investigate too far. Max was a local character, been around for years. The kind who talks your ear off, tells great stories that nobody puts much stock in, and never lets anything important slip. It was pretty clear they thought he'd walked in and surprised a burglar, and dropped dead from shock."

I couldn't believe the kind of man C.D. had described, the kind of man Nannie would have sent me to, could die that way. I stood up, so quickly that I shook the table.

"Where are we going?" C.D. demanded.

"To the hospital. You can come, but I'm going to see my grandmother, and I'm going to see her alone."

It was easier said than done. Monsieur Guillaume had been as good as his word and had had Nannie transferred into a private room with round-the-clock private nurses. She was strung up in traction and hooked to a battery of machines, and nobody was about to leave her unwatched. I had to threaten the combined weight of Monsieur Guillaume, McCausland Industries, and the American embassy before I was finally allowed in by myself, and even so the nurse kept a grim watch through the glass panes in the door.

Nannie looked so small and frail it scared me. Her eyes were closed, and I didn't know whether she was asleep or sedated. I pulled a chair up to the bed, and bent and kissed her.

Instantly, her eyelids struggled open. Her eyes, though clouded, were full of wariness and fear that softened somewhat with relief as she recognized me. "Tori," she said weakly. And then, with a start of apprehension, "You must go home."

"No way," I said firmly. "Especially not now that I know about O.S.S."

Her eyes flared.

"You told me, just before the operation, remember? Don't try to talk," I said quickly. "Just listen. Nannie, I put your jewelry away, do you understand? And I got what you left for me. You, and Granddaddy. They're safe," I said quickly. "They're where you left them." I thought she looked relieved. Her eyelids fluttered.

"Nannie, stay awake, please! I have to tell you something. I found the Fatman—on the street where you were trying to take me shopping. Nan, it was too late." I told her in the same words C.D. had used with me. "The scenario was the same as in our garden. And the set decor the way our place was when I got back from bringing you here the first time."

Nannie's fingers gripped mine. "You *must* go."

"Forget it! I'm going to be all right. I'll make sure. Granddaddy brought me up to be a good ol' girl, remember?" I could tell from Nannie's eyes she wasn't sure whether to be amused or frightened. "I'm going to see that you're all right. And I'll find out the whole truth for you, I swear I will."

"Mademoiselle, you must go now." The nurse came in, bristling starch and authority. I rose and kissed my grandmother.

"I'll be back tomorrow. Is there anything I can bring you?"

"Get the bicarb," Nannie said urgently. I blinked.

"What? Oh, you mean bring some tooth—"

"No. Get the bicarb. Not ours. His. No matter what you have to do. Just get it."

Her eyes blazed with intensity.

"I will. I promise," I said, and kissed her again. And went out to join C.D., thinking hard.

Nannie wanted the Fatman's toothpaste. But why? I told C.D., once we were alone, and he, too, was puzzled.

"We'll get it first, and find out after," he decided.

"How?"

"My first thought is to try to bribe the policemen."

"Forget it. We could land in worse trouble than we are already."

"Okay, then we go to plan two. The kids."

"What?"

"The street kids. They're everywhere, they have eyes in the back of their heads, and they'd never tell the police anything. And I don't believe for one minute they can't get into any building in the city, no matter how well it's locked and guarded. I'll promise one of the little ones *baksheesh* to get the toothpaste for me. I'll ask for a couple of other things, too, photographic things, so he'll think I'm just another black market dealer and won't remember toothpaste. I doubt if he'd know what the stuff is, anyway. And I'll keep a sharp watch to make sure what he brings me comes straight out of Max's place."

So that's what we did. I bought myself another caftan, a green one this time, and wound a scarf around my hair, and I stood bartering for cheap jewelry at one of the street stalls while C.D., doing his annoying American photographer routine, watched from closer in. Within minutes the kid he'd hired was back in triumph. C.D. paid him off and winked at me, and minutes later we came together around the corner.

"Got it," C.D. said, and hailed a cab.

Back in the suite, eating room service dinner once again, we checked the loot. We had the toothpaste, a used, very good German camera with a zoom lens, and a number of rolls of unused 35-millimeter film. C.D. turned the camera over somberly.

"I don't feel like a crook at all pinching this. It was Max's favorite; he'd rather I had it than have it hit the streets. Which is what'll happen with the rest of the stuff. He had no family."

"C.D., I'm sorry."

"Me, too." He put the camera away gently and looked at me. "Okay, Mata Hari. We have the toothpaste. But can you tell me why?"

I had no idea. I knew only one thing. Nannie, however doped up, would never have sent me for it without a reason. Any more than she'd have killed without a reason.

14 The next day was Sunday, and it was a terrible day.

C.D. stayed over in the suite again Saturday night, sprawled on one of the gilt French sofas. They weren't long enough for him, and his legs hung over the carved wood arms. I lay on the bed in my room, with the door ajar, racked with confused emotions.

I was awfully glad C.D. was there, because I was scared. I was relieved that he now knew, if not the whole truth, at least nothing but the truth. Keeping up a pretense had been so darn hard. Being alone with the secrets burning in me had been so very lonely. But I was all too aware that having C.D. just beyond that thin wall was a temptation—to run to him as a security blanket, and a whole lot more. It would be all too easy to spill out the attempt to abduct me, and the awful aftermath. It would be all too easy to let other barriers down as well. After all the emotion C.D. and I had shared, I was very conscious that he was, as he'd put it, not a total clown.

Thinking about C.D. kept me from thinking about Nannie. But I had to think about Nannie. How to keep a secret the fact that she'd killed. Suppose she mumbled something while under drugs or anesthesia—what could I do? Suppose the police had found the body and were quietly putting two and two together—the man dying outside

Nannie's door, the snake in her suite, and the body around the corner from where she'd been run down.

That body couldn't just have vanished, could it, even in Morocco? What would the police make of that puncture in the neck? How had Nannie done that?

C.D.'s being there meant I couldn't go on reading Nannie's letter, which I'd locked away in what I hoped was safety. I lay there in my thin nightgown, tossing and turning. Every sound outside, every creak in the corridor made me start, wondering if I should have kept the loaded gun with me in the suite. By morning I was loopy from lack of sleep, and my head was splitting.

C.D. took one look at me and said firmly, "Take a shower and get dressed. We're getting out of here."

"What?"

"The hotel serves breakfast out by the pool. You've been holed up in this room too much. After that we're going out somewhere. Someplace with people. There's safety in numbers, supposedly."

"I have to see Nannie. And we have to—to try to see the pattern in what's happening."

"We've been trying to. It's time to give it a rest. Don't you know when you get nowhere, chewing something over? Let all the pieces marinate awhile in your unconscious. And you know the doctors aren't going to let you hang around Nannie all day. They'd tell you you were overstimulating her, and they'd be right. So hurry up and get dressed!"

"Yes, sir!" I barked out, and saluted him. Secretly, though, I had to admit he had a point. We had a breakfast buffet beside the pool, and the fresh air did me good. My head still throbbed, but in a lower key. The ache flared to life again as soon as I went by the front desk. Letters were there for Nannie and me from my parents. They wanted to know how our vacation was, Mama hoped I was meeting some nice young men, and Daddy gave me a lecture about taking care of myself and my aging grandma. They also wanted us to call home, collect, to let them know we were all right.

I wasn't going to tackle that hot potato yet. We went back to the suite and phoned the hospital. Mme. Clay had had as comfortable a night as could be expected, but was under heavy sedation because of pain. It would be best for Mademoiselle not to disturb her. M. Guillaume had called and would be calling Mademoiselle to report.

"I don't want to see him," I said flatly.

"So don't," C.D. said. "Let's get out of here. Just as well, anyway, in case your parents get the idea to phone." I stood uncertainly, and he added, "You might as well come, because while you were reading your mail I paid for two tickets for this morning's guided tour of Tangier, and I doubt if the guy's going to give me my money back."

I let C.D. steer me out of the suite again. Along with a lot of other tourists, we lined up obediently for the bus, and I had to admit it was a good idea. With all the people, and nonstop narrative in French and English, not to mention a guide who treated us all like kindergarteners, I didn't have a chance to think. Besides, it was interesting. The guide, a brisk young Moroccan woman, gave us a rapid-fire account of Tangier history from its settling by the Phoenicians through capture by the Romans in 82 B.C., Arab occupation in A.D. 705, establishment of the kingdom of Morocco at the end of the eighth century, and on through the waves of European occupation—Portuguese, English, French, and Spanish. Tangier had become "international territory" in 1923, administered by a council of Moroccan Moslems, Moroccan Jews, and representatives of several European nations. It stopped being officially international when Morocco became independent in 1956.

"Our king is both our political and religious ruler. Our laws and our criminal justice system are based upon both French law and the Koran, and ignorance of the laws is no defense, whether the transgressor is Moroccan or a foreigner," she said. I shuddered.

The bus let us out at the Grand Socco, the main market, through the medina's main gate, and I started getting flashbacks. Our group passed bloody carcasses hanging in the meat market, and I saw the blood of a dead man, his artery severed. We stopped to watch a snake charmer, and I saw a green snake shooting up from a bathroom drawer; the Coca-Cola sign made me feel again waves of hate. I started to shake, and C.D. took my hand and squeezed it tightly. Then we came to the Casbah, with seventeenth-century York House, built as a fortress for the English governors, and Dar el Maghzen, the old royal palace, now a museum, and things got better.

Dar el Maghzen, with its tiles and filigree, its exquisite intertwined vine carvings and fountains and filtered light, brought me peace. I gave C.D.'s hand a squeeze back, and he smiled, and we wandered, enchanted, as far apart from the rest of our group as the guide would let us go.

The guide was telling the story of the great Mulay Idris ibn Abdallah, who in the eighth century "began here in Tangier the moves that led for the first time to Morocco becoming a separate kingdom." They were tales of great power, great beauty and insight, and at times great cruelty.

"Mulay Idris the First became so powerful, in fact, that the great Caliph Haroun al Rashid found him a threat. In the last decade of the eighth century he sent an agent to infiltrate Idris's court, befriend him, and ultimately eliminate him by poisoning his toothpaste."

Several people snickered at that. Who'd have dreamed people were using toothpaste over a thousand years ago, I thought.

And then I gasped aloud.

I clapped my hand over my mouth as a few people stared at me. C.D. jabbed me sharply in the ribs. His blue eyes blazed, and I knew he had read my mind.

With one accord we crept off from the others as our tour group moved on. "You're thinking what I'm thinking," C.D. said.

I nodded. "It's crazy, but it could just be the truth. Only how—"

"Mademoiselle! M'sieu!" our guide called.

C.D. took my elbow. "We can't do anything here, and we can't leave." He was right; we didn't dare risk making ourselves conspicuous. "Just keep your eyes and ears open."

And our brains working . . . as I followed the guide dutifully through the rest of Dar el Maghzen, piece after piece was falling into place like colored glass in a kaleidoscope. There were still alarming gaps in the picture, but at least I now had an idea what to research.

The tour wound up back in the Grand Socco, where our bus was waiting. "We're leaving the tour now," C.D. told the guide firmly, and steered me off. We walked along Rue de la Liberté to the Place de France and sat down in one of the open-air cafés. We ordered mint tea. We stared at each other.

"I've got to do some research," I said. And then, alarmed, "C.D., where is it?"

C.D. patted his jacket pocket. "I never took it out last night. Where do you suppose we can get things analyzed around here?"

"No way, not without causing flak." I concentrated. "You develop your own pictures. You must know something about chemistry, don't you?"

"Some. Enough for this? I don't know where to start."

"You get the things you think you'll need to do a test. I'm going to do some research on my own." I would not explain. Our tea came, and we drank it quickly. I rose. "See you back at the hotel later," I said, and took off before C.D. could stop me. I was going on a fishing expedition, and having him around could make it harder.

I headed for the Entwhistles' hotel. Fortunately, they were in, about to have a midday Sunday dinner, and they invited me to join them. I discovered I was ravenous. Sometime after hearing about Haroun al Rashid's murder method, my headache had completely vanished.

We went to the hotel's canopied-roof garden restaurant, overlooking Tangier Bay, and I told Mr. Entwhistle

110

I'd gotten so interested in what he'd told me about World War II espionage that I'd decided to do a research paper on it for school next fall. Mr. Entwhistle gave me a pretty shrewd glance, but he asked me no questions, and he did tell me all the stories he could think of.

"The movies make it glamorous, but from what I hear, most of the work was pretty routine," he said.

Mrs. Entwhistle's eyes twinkled. "Pretty routine! That's not the way you told it to me when we were courting!" She turned to me proudly. "He's too modest to tell you, but he was in Military Intelligence himself. That was the armed forces version of the O.S.S. And the stories he used to tell me would curl your hair."

"I'm afraid that was mostly exaggeration to impress you," Mr. Entwhistle said sheepishly. "I found out after the war that a friend of mine had been in O.S.S., and *he* had stories. Ways you could kill without it ever being detected, and so on."

My heart started pounding. "I read something somewhere about killing with a rolled newspaper." *Newspaper*, I said, not *magazine*. He nodded.

"You know how you can cut your finger on an edge of paper. Roll it tight enough, and you have a blade." Yes, I knew. "And then there were undetectable poisons, using an empty hypodermic to shoot an air bubble into the bloodstream, special judo maneuvers. Heck, we see the stuff on TV all the time now. But it's real. My friend said they were taught many different techniques before they were sent into the field. For emergency use only. But that most assassins developed one favorite method, which became a trademark, identifiable as a fingerprint. I believe the police find the same pattern among organized crime figures. The C.I.A.'s probably familiar with it, too."

I wet my lips. "I don't suppose you know how to test for those rare poisons."

Mr. Entwhistle grinned. "That's my wife's department. She used to be a pharmacist with the Poison Control Bureau," he said to my stupefaction. "Tell her, Doris."

Talk about coincidences. It was about time one worked in my favor. I scribbled frantically as Mrs. Entwhistle, rather amused to be talking shop, rattled through a lot of technical information.

We ate a large and very good dinner. We had fabulous desserts. I finally managed with difficulty to get away, amid a chorus of good wishes for Nannie.

I went to the hospital and got in to see my grandmother, who was weak and in pain, but conscious.

"I'm much better, darling," she murmured calmly, but her eyes asked urgent questions.

"I got what you asked me to get," I said. "And I figured out why it was important. Nan, I've been doing research—for that paper I told you I'm going to write for my senior project. Will you take a look and tell me whether any of these are the right procedures?"

I held the notes I'd taken close before her face.

Nannie's eyes started with recognition. Then, very carefully, one of her fingers traced on the counterpane the number three. *The third test.*

"You mean the third way would be best?" I asked, and she nodded.

"You shouldn't—Tori, you should go home."

"No way. Unless you really want your son, and probably your daughter-in-law, jetting over here to take over. They'd probably load you on a plane, too, and fly you back. Are you really ready to leave Morocco, with all your—unfinished business here? By the way, we both got letters from them. They're antsy 'cause they haven't heard from us. I'll think of a way to stall them. Guillaume's not going to spill the beans. He's too worried about publicity. So much so that he's persuaded the hospital to be afraid of publicity, too. So no one knows you're here."

That wasn't quite true, but it reassured Nannie, and the few people who did know weren't going to let things leak.

"Tori," my grandmother whispered. "The letter . . ."

"I haven't had time to finish it. Please, Nan, don't worry."

It was easy to say, but I had an uneasy certainty that reading the rest of that letter was going to be like uncovering a whole basketful of cobras.

I kissed Nannie, and said good-bye just in time to escape another lecture from her nurse. Back at the suite C.D. was waiting impatiently.

"Don't disappear like that again. I didn't know *what* might have happened to you!"

"I'm back in one piece. And I've got the formula to test the toothpaste. Don't ask me to go through how I got it." I passed my notes over, with the third formula circled. "We can try the other ones, too, if number three shows nothing. But I'm sure this is it."

C.D. set up a lab in the bigger bathroom, after we'd shoved Nannie's cosmetics out of the way. How he'd acquired equipment like a Bunsen burner I didn't ask. We performed the steps of the test and waited with drawn breath.

The telltale clouded stain began to creep up the side of the laboratory flask. I gave an involuntary sound. "We did it! We really did it," I exclaimed excitedly. And turned, to find C.D. behind me in the act of leaning down.

Our lips met by accident, but it wasn't accidentally that they stayed together. "I think that's enough chemistry for now," I whispered shakily as we drew apart.

"Yeah. Right. There's too much we need to concentrate on right this minute." C.D. thrust his hands into his pockets and paced, as though afraid to risk getting too close again. "Let's go back through this logically. We know the toothpaste's poisoned, though I don't know the name of the poison and I bet you don't, either. Wait a minute. Maybe we'd better make sure what we found *is* poison."

He spread some of the toothpaste, carefully, with one of the lab spatulas he'd gotten, onto a slice of the fruit the management provided daily. Then he opened the garden door and set it on a stone. Within a minute a fly had settled greedily. Within another minute the fly was dead.

"That settles it. Somebody planted poison in Max's toothpaste, and somebody probably used the same stuff on Hector Alvarez. I'd give a lot to know whether there were any photos of Hector around Max's place," C.D. said. "There's got to be a link." Using his handkerchief to protect his fingers, he put the cap back on the toothpaste, placed the tube in an envelope, and sealed it. "You'd better put this stuff in your safe deposit box while we decide what to do next."

"I think what we do next is we each write up an account of all this, and we mail it home. You to yourself at your house. Me to—to my grandmother's. Her mail's being held at the post office till she gets back. Then there'll be a written record if—"

I could not go on. *If anything happens to us. Anything more.*

"What I don't understand," C.D. said, "is why, now that we know about this stuff, anybody went to the extreme of planting that snake. Why didn't they just doctor your toothpaste if they wanted to kill you?"

"Because we didn't have any toothpaste, remember? We still don't!" I started to laugh. "Can you imagine someone sneaking in here, not finding a convenient tube? He must have gone crazy trying to find a poisonous snake on such short notice!"

"Tori!" C.D. said in alarm. "We don't have time for you to get hysterical giggles. We still don't know the main thing. *Why* were these people killed? Why is someone trying to kill you and your grandmother?"

The questions stopped my laughter more quickly than a lecture. "I don't know," I said soberly. "But I think I know where I'll find out."

15 I had to read the rest of Nannie's letter, and I knew it. I put it off as long as I could, through dinner and a long silent session during which C.D. and I each wrote our separate accounts. We sealed them and wrote our names across the seals, as Nannie had done. Tomorrow I'd arrange through M. Guillaume to send them to the States by overnight air delivery.

C.D. announced his intention to spend the night again. "Aren't you ever going to get your money's worth from your own hotel?" I asked. C.D. shook his head.

"Not till I know you're safe. Look, do you think your grandmother'd mind if I used her bed? Hanging my six feet over a five-foot sofa's beginning to get me down."

"Sure, why not. First let's go lock these epistles up." I went to the safe deposit box, with C.D. escorting me as bodyguard and waiting outside the cubicle. I didn't just put the envelopes in, I took Nannie's letter and the gun back out. But I didn't say so. We went back to the suite, where C.D. kissed me good-night with deliberate lightness, and I went to bed. As soon as I was reasonably sure he was asleep, I got up again.

I put on my dark caftan and made sure the draperies at the windows were tightly shut. Then I turned on a lamp in the sitting room and curled up on a sofa. I didn't want to be in my room alone, with C.D. the whole width of the suite away.

And I read the rest of Nannie's letter.

> The Jaguar had gone out in such haste that an oil lamp still burned on his table, and the book he'd been writing in was still open. . . . It was his private diary, and it was in code. . . .

Even though Nannie was in love with the Jaguar, her O.S.S. training had taken over. She could decipher codes. And what she read, in those few moments by the sputtering lamplight, had devastated her.

> Jaguar was the mole. A double agent, collaborating with the Nazis. I stayed there only long enough to see that much. My feet had turned to stone. But I knew what I had to do.

Somehow, she'd gotten out of the little room with no one seeing, taking the journal with her. She'd fled back to her own lodging, and sat up all night, decoding feverishly. And by morning the Nance O'Neill she'd been till now, the young girl living a patriotic adventure filled with grand passions, was no more.

The Jaguar had been responsible for her British soldier's death. Personally responsible. And responsible for her not having been there, too, the night of the explosion.

> Something in me died. It was a ghost—no, a woman early old—who kept on going. I'd been well trained. I knew I had to pass the information on to my control.

That was her superior, one of the few persons in the Underground whose rank she knew. She knew none of them by their real names. It was sheer chance—the fact that she had a civilian trade, fashion photography, that could be capitalized on—that had caused her to be known by her real name, Nance O'Neill.

I could not stay in Tangier any longer. I was too afraid the Jaguar could trace the journal's disappearance to me, and I could not put it back. It might be needed. I memorized as much of it as I could, and I went to one of my French Underground contacts. I knew him only as the Fatman. I left all my clothes, my camera, personal belongings—if the Jaguar came looking, he'd think something had happened to me. Life was cheap in those days. He himself had had to take out a German agent with his favorite method. A kind of poison with no taste. In toothpaste, or anything else that came in contact with the mucus membranes, it would be absorbed into the bloodstream and become undetectable. Within hours it would induce an enormous, and fatal, heart attack.

Tori darling, the Jaguar and I had shared toothpaste and a few things more. I wasn't going to give him a chance to take me out.

She had gone to the Fatman, and the Fatman had arranged to have her smuggled that night across the Strait of Gibraltar and into Spain. The night had been stormy, and there was always danger of mines in the water. She hadn't dared risk carrying the journal with her.

I left it with the Fatman. I knew the O.S.S. would find a way to get it, after the war, if not before. I managed to get to England, and I reported to Military Intelligence headquarters in London—once I could get in to see them.

They patted me on the head and said good show, they'd take care of things from there, and sent me back to my fashion magazine in London. I couldn't get back home. I worked for the magazine, and the O.S.S. when they had something I could do in some back office, like decoding cables. And I met your grandfather. And after the war, I heard the Jaguar had been killed in action. So the truth about him, and about Paul, never came out. There seemed no reason.

And Nance O'Neill was no more.

Tori darling, forgive me for not telling you all this. I have to hope you're woman enough to understand why. Forgive me for burdening you with it now. If you're reading this, something will have happened, and it is necessary for you to know these things, because your own life is in danger. Not for something you happened to photograph, my darling. Because you're with me.

I don't know where the journal is. I don't know where the Fatman is. Perhaps dead. The man called Hector Alvarez was a member of the French Underground. I never did know his name, but I'm sure it wasn't Alvarez. He must have come to warn me. Perhaps the Fatman sent him.

The snake wasn't planted for you. It was meant for me. It was probably put in your bathroom by mistake, because whoever brought it thought the old woman, not the young, would be the one with a bathroom with no cosmetics.

It's late, and I am very tired. I can't write more. The rest will have to wait till I can tell you. I hope to God I'll never have to.

God be with you, darling,
Nannie

I sat staring at the paper through eyes blurred with tears. Blurred though my real vision was, my inner sight was clear. And what I saw made me cold.

It wasn't just that Nannie had kept secrets, that she'd had a whole other life. She'd lied to me. We hadn't come here because she was giving me an out from the deb party, or because she felt nostalgic. She'd come to find the Jaguar's journal. I'd only been her cover. She'd been using me.

My funny, charming executive-wife grandmother was a killer. She'd killed in wartime—I was sure of that, though she didn't say it—and she'd killed again. I knew she'd done it to save me—*from a situation she'd gotten me into*, an outraged voice inside me whispered; *somebody was trying to get at her through me. Or thought I had the journal—*

I knew being a government agent, one of the "good guys," was supposed to justify her actions. But I couldn't buy it. Everything I'd learned since coming here went counter to everything I'd been taught—and taught by her. I was flesh of her flesh, blood of her blood, and we were strangers.

Something else, something not personal, kept intruding on my pain and rage. War crimes had no statute of limitations. Somebody knew Mrs. Henry McCausland Clay was Nance O'Neill, O.S.S. agent, and was afraid of what she knew. *That* was why all these things had happened.

We came to Tangier, and two men died. Nannie still might die. And me.

I sat there like a statue, like one of the dolls in the bazaar. My left hand held the letter. My right hand, as if it were searching for security, closed around Granddaddy's silver-trimmed revolver.

Something brushed my neck, and I screamed. The gun came up as I fought and kicked, and someone gripped me.

C.D. was shaking me. C.D. was shouting my name. *"Tori! Look at me! It's ME!"*

My vision cleared, and then I collapsed into his arms.

16 "You've got to tell me everything," C.D. said. "This is getting too dangerous for both of us." Again, he'd gotten brandy and made me drink it. Now he sat, facing me on the sofa, carefully not touching.

"My gosh, Tori, all I did was kiss the back of your neck, and you went berserk. You reacted as if I were trying to kill you! And you knew you were safe in here—it's locked up like a fortress, and I'm on guard."

"Somebody *did* try to kill me," I said thickly. All my barriers were tumbling down.

C.D.'s *"What?"* was a very satisfactory reaction.

"The other night. Right before the—the accident. Nannie and I were walking home from a restaurant, and we were followed. Carefully. The—the shadow merged with ours. And then it—he—grabbed me."

C.D. made a shocked, involuntary exclamation and I put my arm out blindly. "No! Let me finish. He grabbed me, and—and Nannie killed him."

The room was so still, I thought I could hear the pounding of our hearts.

"Start at the beginning," C.D. said carefully, "and tell me all of it. Piece by piece."

So I did. All of it. By the time I was finished, I was in his arms, and he was stroking my hair gently.

"Thank God for your grandmother," he said softly.

"I know. But I—can't accept it. And then she—she was deliberately run down."

"She's safer in the hospital than anywhere," C.D. said. "Unless we can persuade the doctors to let us bring her here. Either way, we can get guards. McCausland Industries can do that, can't they? Or you should go to the American embassy."

"And tell them what? Excuse me, but my grandmother the ex-secret agent killed somebody. The body's disappeared, so we have no proof. You heard what the guide said about the Moroccan criminal code."

C.D. ran his fingers through his hair. "There must be a loophole somewhere. . . . You're right, it must be that journal everybody's after. We'll just have to find it. If we turn it over to the authorities, that should put a stop to everything."

"Ha!" I said bitterly. "Finding a needle in a haystack's a picnic compared to finding something hid in wartime, forty-five or more years ago!"

"Maybe not," C.D. said thoughtfully. "I think I know where the diary could be."

Now it was my turn to say *"What?!"*

"Max told me about a friend he had, the kind who didn't ask or answer questions. I know I said Max was the kind of guy who told great stories but no real facts, but your grandmother says the Fatman was part of the Underground. One of the things secret agents are taught is always to stick to the truth as much as possible. It makes trip-ups less likely. We were talking once about the drug trade—you know a lot of hashish passes through Morocco—and Max laughed and said he'd bet anything his pal

123

Hassan was involved in that. That Hassan was the ideal courier, because he saw and heard everything, and didn't give a thing away; he could deal with both sides, and no matter what happened, Hassan would come out okay. And he said Hassan had the perfect cover, the ideal situation for concealing things."

"What was it?" I asked mechanically.

"He owned a pottery shop. If Alvarez was trying to warn your grandmother, the Fatman *had* to have known what was up. Maybe he sent Alvarez to her. And if he stashed that journal somewhere, then or now, I'm positive it would be with his pal Hassan."

"There's just one problem," I pointed out. "We don't know where Hassan is."

"Yes, we do," C.D. said smugly. "In Marrakech." He drew me to my feet. "Go to bed, my child, and dream about pottery amphora. First thing in the morning, I'll get us on a tour to Marrakech."

I slept better than I had any night so far.

C.D. was as good as his word, and at nine Monday morning we were again aboard a tour bus. This time the guide was a man—small, dapper, French. The bus was crowded, mostly with Japanese tourists.

The ride to Marrakech was uneventful. Fortunately, the bus was air-conditioned. Remembering Nannie's lecture on proper clothes for women in Moslem countries, I was wearing a navy shift with sleeves, one of Nannie's big-brimmed hats, and sandals. And I carried Granddaddy's gun in Nannie's purse. C.D. was loaded down with cameras, including Max's.

We stopped twice en route, once for shopping and once

to give us a chance, at extra charge, to ride some sad-looking camels. One was white, and a baby, and C.D. took my picture with it. "Don't you want to ride?" he suggested.

"I get plenty of riding back in Texas. On nice, sensible horses." One of the camels spit in C.D.'s face at that moment, and I snickered.

Marrakech, said the guide, conjured up dreams of caravans and palm trees, merciless combats and romantic honeymoons. Or of international espionage. I dropped my gaze.

The medina of Marrakech covered more than two square miles, and one could lose oneself there very easily, he explained. Marrakech's most famous landmark was the Koutoubia minaret, which thrust proudly up into the sky. He called our attention to it when it appeared, and the other tourists obediently snapped pictures. C.D. did, too, so we wouldn't call attention to ourselves by being different.

We already had our game plan set. Once we were in the medina, we would ditch the tour. We were going to pretend we were slipping off to be alone. The entrance to the Grand Souk was impressive, a series of keyhole-shaped arches. We followed the rest of the tour group off the bus and put our plan in action.

I started a good imitation of Sue Hopper when she's trying to get a guy to spend money on her, talking about all that cute jewelry in the souk displays. C.D. pretended to be holding out, then weakening. He got our guide aside and asked for recommendations to good jewelry shops. The guide was enchanted to be of help. Probably in hope of kickbacks from the stores, I thought. Before we left him, we had him convinced it was jewelry we were seeking—but we'd also found out which area of the medina housed the pottery shops.

I was afraid to hope. But there *is* a providence. The fourth Hassan the Potter that we came to was the right one. Yes, he was a friend of Fat Max, the photograph gallery owner in Tangier. Fat Max had sent us? We must sit and have mint tea.

"I am delighted to be of service to one of Max's friends." Hassan rubbed his hands together. "And to Mademoiselle Clay, yes?"

I started.

"Yes, as a matter of fact, but how did you know?" C.D. demanded.

"I saw an excellent photograph in the English-language newspaper last week," Hassan said blandly. "Mademoiselle Clay and Madame McCausland Clay. All businessmen are aware of McCausland Industries, and I am a businessman."

I'll bet you are, I thought, noting the diamond rings on his yellowed hands. He didn't say a word about Nance O'Neill.

"How is my friend Max?" he asked, busily serving the steaming mint tea in tall glasses.

"Max is dead," C.D. said bluntly. "A heart attack. The police *say*."

"Ahhh." Hassan drew his breath in with a hiss, but the old hands, passing a glass to me, never faltered. He sat, picking up his own glass to salute us. "How may I serve you, m'sieu? Mademoiselle?"

I made a daring gamble. "You are keeping a package for my grandmother, are you not? From forty-five years ago. I've come for it."

For a minute there was no sound except the gentle jangle of the brass wind chimes. Then Hassan gave another little hiss.

"I had wondered. Mademoiselle, you are astute. Because of Max, I will give it to you, and may the praise or blame rest with Allah. I will need a few moments; it is sealed away. Be so good as to sit here and drink your tea."

He rose, nodding his head over his folded hands, and went to the rear of the shop. C.D. caught my eye and jerked his head. We could just see Hassan's reflection in a brass-framed mirror. He was behind a partition, climbing a ladder to move some dusty old amphorae on an upper shelf—those ancient-looking pottery jars with the round bodies and double handles.

From behind them he produced another amphora, older, sealed, and started down the ladder. As he did so, a string of bells at the shop's front entrance jingled.

My back was to the doorway, but I could see it reflected in another mirror. The back of my neck began to prickle. A handsome black-haired young European was coming in. A familiar-looking young man.

"C.D.," I whispered.

C.D. reacted instantly. He rose, calling, "Thanks for the tea, mate," in an Irish accent. He took my arm. We moved out of sight into the back of the shop, managing to move the mirror that showed it as we did so. C.D. took the amphora from Hassan's hands and jerked his head toward the front of the store, and Hassan bustled out, already starting his sales pitch as he did so. Then C.D. grabbed my hand and pulled me with him out of the shop's back door.

We were in a narrow, damp-floored corridor running behind rows of shops. "Duck in one of them and swipe some djellabas," he ordered, and I did so without batting an eye. No one saw me. I was back in a flash, to find C.D. bending over a pile of broken pottery shards.

"Got it," he whispered, scooping up a waterstained brown leather notebook.

In an instant we were running down the corridor, hand in hand. We stopped before its end, breathing hard, and pulled on the hooded robes. I pushed the hood of my djellaba up over my head to hide my hair. "You'd better, too," I gasped, thinking of C.D.'s noticeable orange head. C.D. obeyed.

We emerged into one of the main streets of the medina. I had Nannie's handbag over my shoulder, inside the djellaba, and I kept my head down to hide my face. I knew now that others beside Hassan might have seen that picture.

We faked a saunter, pretending to be shoppers. C.D. could be nothing but American—or possibly Irish—but I hoped I had a chance of looking native. My hair was dark, and I was very tanned. Maybe if I put on some kohl . . . I bought makeup, and smudged the black kohl around my eyes hastily. It was amazing the difference that it made.

Our guide had given orders: anyone who got separated from the group was to meet the others by the bus, in front of the keyhole arch. We could just see it in the distance when I became conscious of a pattern in the footsteps to our rear.

They were even footsteps, of someone wearing heavy shoes. Not sandals. I caught C.D.'s eye, and he nodded imperceptibly and picked up speed. The footsteps did, too.

We were nearing a busy part of the market now. We slowed.

The footsteps slowed also, staying a measured number of yards behind.

17 "Come on," C.D. muttered grimly. "We're getting out of here!" We picked up speed and pushed through throngs of shoppers. For moments at a time, we could not hear those measured footsteps. Then, always, they came again, ever nearer.

There were side passages we could duck into, but there we might be alone. There was more safety in numbers, surely. I glanced fearfully at C.D. and saw that he felt the same. We dared not turn around and look—there was always the chance that, in our djellabas, our identities might be in doubt. Just the sliver of a chance—but we needed every edge.

We turned a corner, and in a shop window as we turned I caught a backward glimpse. It was the man who'd come into Hassan's shop. And he was gaining on us.

"C.D.," I breathed, and C.D.'s voice whispered sternly, "I know. Keep quiet." His hand gripped my elbow and hurried me along.

We were in sight of the keyhole arch now. I began to run, bumping into people, holding the hood of the djellaba close against my face.

We were out into the sunlight. I could not hear the footsteps. And there was the bus, waiting.

C.D.'s arm swept around my waist and carried me along. My lungs hurting, we stumbled over—

The bus was empty. The door was tightly shut.

I almost cried out in dismay, and C.D.'s hand went across my mouth. I nodded, and he released me. He was right. The worst thing to do was call attention to ourselves. We groped our way over to the fringes of a crowd of strangers. A snake charmer again, I noticed giddily.

And then I heard them, almost soundless, right behind me. Those footsteps—by now my heightened hearing could not mistake the particular creak of leather with each left step. I literally felt the man's breath on my neck. I stiffened and reached for C.D.'s hand, for he had not noticed.

It wasn't C.D.'s hand that closed on mine.

And then, in the nick of time, the marines arrived. The marines, in the person of our loud and talkative guide. Leading his troupe of tourists, brandishing the walking stick he used to get attention, he brayed, *"Ah, les jeunes amoureux!"* and came charging over.

Les jeunes amoureux ... the young lovers ... I absolutely loved him at that moment, because the hand, the footsteps, were no longer there. They had dissolved into the crowd, leaving me sure that if the guide had come one second later, he would have found me dead. It was not only toothpaste and rolled papers that could kill swiftly, silently, unnoticed in a crowd. What had Mr. Entwhistle said about hypodermic needles filled with air?

I think for a minute I passed out. I wasn't sure, because C.D. was holding me up. The next thing I saw was C.D.'s look of concern, his bafflement.

I whispered an explanation to him later, my lips close to his ear as we jounced along in the air-conditioned bus.

The rest of the passengers were sure by now that we were totally absorbed in each other, and we let them think so. It was our only cover, the only way that we could talk. There *are* times when deception is necessary, I told myself . . . or was it all deception?

We didn't get back to Tangier till long after midnight, for the journey was lengthy and again we stopped twice, once for a couscous dinner in a "native tent"—brass platters, an old man playing pipes, harem dancers, and more camels—and once to view desert and mountains in the moonlight. C.D. kissed me there; he had kissed me several times on the bus, as a matter of fact, but not like that time at the hotel. It was—comfortable. Peaceful. As if we'd known each other for a lifetime.

In a weird sort of way, we had.

The tour bus let us off at the door of the Hotel Grande, and we crept inside. The night clerk nodded, and I realized he must have accepted the fact that C.D. was staying with me with my grandmother away. Oh, well, I thought, let him think what he wants. My key ring was in Nannie's purse, and I had to grope around for it; C.D. was holding our new djellabas and couldn't get to his key. My fingers found the Jaguar's journal, the kohl I'd bought, Granddaddy's gun. And finally the keys. I remember we were snickering slightly as I brought them out, because by now we were in the slaphappy stage of weariness and relief.

I turned the key in the lock, and we started to step inside. And then I froze. I knew with absolute certainty, but no proof at all, that an intruder had been inside—and might still be there.

I backed off quickly, so quickly I bumped into C.D.

who, catching my tension, shifted quickly and made no sound. I eased the door shut and withdrew the key. C.D. jerked his head toward the corridor leading to the pool, and we crept out there.

I slid around the wall of the pool terrace, like Nannie and I had done that first night when Alvarez knocked, and C.D. copied my every move. At last we were at the nail-studded door that led out to the street.

"Stay in here," C.D. whispered. "I'll get a cab." I nodded. I sought and found the gun and flicked the safety catch off, just in case. My fingers were still locked around the hand grip when C.D. reappeared.

We didn't discuss where we were going. C.D. simply directed the driver to his own hotel, which was quite a distance from the medina, and we went up to his room. It wasn't much, compared to the Hotel Grande suite, but it was clean. It was small, and there was just one single bed. I slept on that while C.D. slept on the floor. That was much later, though.

The journal was burning like acid in my mind, and as soon as C.D. had closed the window shutters, I got it out.

It wasn't all in code. But the parts that weren't— "It's in German," I said despairingly, and could have cried. Which was ridiculous. What had I hoped to find, anyway—a confession?

"I've taken some German," C.D. said. "Let me see."

He looked, turning pages slowly with careful fingers, and an odd expression crept across his face.

"What is it?" I asked half fearfully.

"The guy was in love," C.D. said gently. "And I don't think he was very happy. He was very circumspect, but—

Tori, there's no doubt about it. He had to be talking about Nance O'Neill. There are little references to going to fashion shows with her, to carrying her camera, to black coronet braids."

I nodded, feeling sick. And at the same time, in a strange way, relieved. Nannie hadn't been lying in that letter. I hadn't realized till now that I'd half wanted to believe she had. I had again that queer feeling that I was stepping back through time and knowing Nannie as my peer, my contemporary, a young girl in danger, frightened and confused and swept by passions she did not understand.

And I was haunted by something else as well. A conviction Nannie knew the Jaguar's real identity, and hadn't told.

18 In the morning we went back to the Hotel Grande. I stopped at the desk and said I was sure someone had been in the suite, and the assistant manager went with us and stayed by me as we searched. There was no sign of disturbance. Everything was too perfect.

"Perhaps Mademoiselle's nerves are playing tricks on her," the assistant manager suggested suavely. I bit back a retort. He didn't know. At least, I hoped he didn't know.

A porter brought mail and messages from the desk. A secretary at the American embassy had telephoned to inquire whether Mme. and Mlle. Clay would be attending the gala in Rabat. My mother had called. Fortunately, in both cases the switchboard had said merely that neither Mademoiselle nor Madame were at present in their rooms. Monsieur Guillaume had called repeatedly.

As soon as we got rid of the porter I phoned Monsieur Guillaume and got his secretary. M. Guillaume was in an important business meeting, but would return my call. Instead, he appeared in midmorning. He looked perturbed. "I tried to reach you all day yesterday. I left word for you to call. Did you not get my messages?"

"I was taking a tour and didn't get back till too late to call," I said glibly. Lying was coming more and more easily to me. "Is something wrong? Not Nannie—"

"No, no! I saw Madame yesterday afternoon and she

was resting comfortably," he said hastily. "But some of the things she said disturbed me greatly." He actually wrung his hands while I held my breath.

"Mademoiselle Victoire, I don't wish to alarm you, but something extremely strange is going on. Madame Clay asked me about an incident she'd heard of, the death by heart attack of an expatriate Briton. Maximilian Starr. She said that you had been by his studio, and had told her of it, and that she believed Starr was an acquaintance of her husband's. She wished to know about funeral arrangements so she could send flowers."

C.D. and I carefully avoided exchanging glances.

"She also told me about the frights you had both had here. I was appalled! You should have sent for me at once." I started to say Nannie hadn't wanted him disturbed, but Monsieur Guillaume was hurrying on. "Mademoiselle Victoire, this is my dilemma. I did not want to tell your grandmother because of her condition, but when she mentioned the name of Hector Alvarez I was *most* alarmed."

"Why?" I asked as casually as I could. "We didn't know him. And he—what happened to him—well, it was out in the garden, not in here."

"Yes, but a massive heart attack, so exactly similar to the way Starr expired." How did he know that, I wondered. Guillaume wrung his hands again and came to a decision. "I did not tell Madame Clay, but I have reason to know Starr and Alvarez were connected. In an unsavory way. And then with the Alvarez death never being reported in the papers—"

"Connected how?" C.D. demanded bluntly.

"Not to put too fine a point on it, industrial espionage. The Alvarez person was a wholesaler of this and that, including—so McCausland Industries has reason to suspect—trade secrets. You understand, some of the things we manufacture . . . in order to keep the process and components confidential, we do not even risk applying for patents. We have had secrets stolen, a possibility of documents copied. . . . Starr traveled everywhere with his camera. He had been seen under suspicious circumstances with Alvarez."

Get to the point, I wanted to shout. At the same time, a curious trickle of relief started through me. Maybe the deaths, the attempted deaths, had nothing to do with the Jaguar at all?

"So," Monsieur Guillaume wound up finally, "I went to the gendarmes. McCausland Industries is well known, not a firm to be brushed off frivolously. I laid my suspicions before the police, and the police agreed there could be a connection between the deaths. They pointed out that there are many unexplained deaths in the city, but—" He shrugged. "It is my feeling they are looking into these two heart attacks, and that that is why there has been so little in the papers. I did not say so. I said that Madame Clay, being the widow of Henri McCausland Clay, may know something, may have seen something, and that could be the reason for the attacks on her. I feel very strongly she should have protection."

"So do I," I said through parched lips.

"Good. Because I have already arranged to station some of our bonded security police to stand guard outside her hospital room. With your approval, I will have her transferred today to a private British hospital here. It is run by an Anglican religious order, and McCausland Industries has made substantial contributions to it."

"That sounds fine."

"Then I will leave at once to make arrangements." Monsieur Guillaume bowed. "I will return as soon as I have done so. I would not be surprised if the gendarmes pay a visit to you in the meantime."

It occurred to me they might have already done so, that they could have been the intruders in the suite. I didn't say so. I didn't tell Monsieur Guillaume about that scare, or about what happened in Marrakech yesterday.

He left. C.D. and I searched the suite again. We found nothing. We wouldn't, if the police had been there. Or professional industrial thieves. Somehow I was clinging to that new explanation.

"While we're waiting for Jack-in-the-box to come back," C.D. said, referring to Monsieur Guillaume's frequent bowing, "let's take another look at those pictures you shot in the medina." We spread them out. Something in me tightened.

"C.D., have you got a magnifying glass?"

"I've got this." He produced a jeweler's loupe, the kind photographers and editors use to examine strips of thirty-five-millimeter film. I gazed hard at the photographs, and then I pointed.

"See that guy in the background? Right outside Max's shop? That's the guy who was following us in Marrakech."

"Are you sure?"

"Positive. I got a good look in the mirror when he came

into Hassan's shop." I frowned. "I still don't know why he looked familiar. Darn."

"Probably your subconscious remembered him from these photographs," C.D. said soothingly.

There was no point waiting around in there, not when we were both ready to jump out of our skins. I phoned the hospital and got to speak to Nannie; told her that I'd seen Monsieur Guillaume and that C.D. and I had had a "very exciting" trip to Marrakech yesterday, that while there I'd "bought a book I thought she would enjoy." Nannie responded with her legendary cool. She sounded stronger than the last time I'd seen her. After that C.D. and I went for a swim and had lunch by the pool.

Monsieur Guillaume found us there in midafternoon and herded us to the suite. He looked full of secrets, and he'd rigged up an elaborate plot. In two hours, Nannie would be "discharged" from the hospital and "returned to her hotel." Only it would be C.D., rigged up in bandages, who would actually be transported by ambulance to the Hotel Grande. Another, duplicate ambulance would meanwhile be transporting Nannie to the private hospital under guard.

"I'm riding with her," I said firmly, and would not be talked out of it by Monsieur Guillaume, who thought I ought to be with C.D., putting on an act. Then something struck me. "One more thing. Has any information leaked out so far about Nannie's accident?"

"Certainly not," Monsieur Guillaume said. I thought I saw a flicker of doubt in his eyes.

"Release the story," I said with decision. "Only don't say how bad the accident really was. Say she's well on the way to recovery. And—and get the police to stake out this suite." I saw respect growing in his eyes. "You can get me another room to stay in here, can't you? Say your wife's going to use it to be near me, or something. No," I added hastily, "she won't really. It will just be a story."

"Mademoiselle, you have inherited your grandfather's brilliance. I shall do just as you suggest."

So that's the way we played it, an elaborate charade. I felt almost as if I were a kid again playing pretend. The role-playing came as easily as it had back then. That would have been funny if the stakes were not so high.

Monsieur Guillaume got the key to the new room, and C.D. transferred some clothes there for me. Then Guillaume drove us both to the hospital for the big switch. He had a doctor from the private hospital there, who swathed C.D. in bandages like a mummy. A head scarf and dark glasses completed the transformation. The ambulance hauled C.D. off, along with a female security guard dressed as a nurse. By this point, things were going so smoothly that Monsieur Guillaume and C.D. were having a high old time playing make-believe. I could have killed them.

Nannie and I went into another ambulance, with the doctor and a real nurse and another camouflaged guard. And Monsieur Guillaume. With all of them present, I couldn't really talk to Nannie. But her eyes were alert and bright. I burbled about what a great adventure C.D. and I had had in Marrakech, and I held my—her—bag open in front of her so she could glance inside. She saw the leather-bound journal, her eyes widened, and she nodded imperceptibly. Yes; that was it. She saw the gun, and looked alarmed.

"Everything's okay," I said swiftly. "I just need to know what—what I should do with the gift I brought you."

"Send it back to the States," Nannie said. "Be sure it's carefully packed."

"Maybe I could get your old employers to do it." I meant the American embassy, or the consulate, and she knew it. When she was settled in her new hospital room, she scribbled a brief note for me to take. "Show them that. They'll take care of it." I thrust the note in my wallet quickly.

"I'll do it right away."

My voice sounded unnatural, and of course she knew it. Her thin hand rested on my arm. "Dear Tori. I'm so sorry. For everything."

"Don't be," I said gruffly. "We all . . . do what we have to do."

" 'To every thing there is a season.' We'll talk about it—soon. Please. I promise."

I nodded, and then I had to leave.

I knew that quote. "To every thing there is a season, and a time to every purpose under heaven." A time to be born and a time to die—but deaths by murder weren't God's "right time." And a time to betray? A time to hide truths? A time to lie?

I loved Nannie, I still loved Nannie, but not the same way, and I didn't know whether I ever would. I was hiding truths and telling lies myself, I had to, but I didn't know whether I could forgive myself.

19   I went back to the Hotel Grande, but I didn't go to the suite or to my new room. I accessed our safe deposit box and took out my passport, which I thought I might need as identification at the consulate. The accounts C.D. and I had written still lay there. I took those out, too, and after careful thought returned Granddaddy's gun to the box. I might get in trouble taking that to the consulate.

I handed the safe deposit box back to the manager, and explained that I needed to make copies of some documents. Could I use his secretary's duplicating machine?

The manager was eager to be of service. His secretary would do the job for me herself. "No!" I said hastily. "No, I'll do it. I know how." The secretary, who had been listening, looked relieved. She showed me into a little room and I closed the door behind me.

I made copies of the accounts C.D. and I had written, helped myself to two fresh envelopes from a supply shelf, and addressed them, then put the original accounts inside and sealed them up. I made a copy of the entire diary. I put the original of that in an envelope, too. Then I got into the safe deposit box again—the manager's patience was wearing thin—and stashed away all my photocopies.

And I took the original documents to the American consulate. I found the address in an English-language directory the secretary had. I didn't say what I was looking for, and I didn't tell C.D. where I was going. There were some things I just had to do myself. Besides, I needed space. I felt as though I were suffocating.

I had some trouble getting in to see anybody important at the consulate, but at last the McCausland Clay name worked magic. I produced my passport—for the third time since arrival—and handed over Nannie's scribbled note. *That* got results. The man who read it started, and began making interoffice phone calls. A couple of discreet and official-looking men in dark suits appeared, and a young man and woman in military uniforms.

"We know who your grandmother is, Miss Clay," the older of the officials said. I just bet he did, and that it wasn't as Granddaddy's widow. "How may we be of service?"

I produced my sealed packets. "My grandmother wants these to go to the States by the safest possible means. And the fastest." At first I thought they were going to balk at the envelopes being sealed, or at their going to Nannie's home address. Then the same man cut through the red tape. A large mailing envelope was produced, my items were put in it, and the envelope addressed. To Nannie's home; I checked.

"This will go out in tonight's diplomatic pouch and be forwarded immediately from Washington."

I had a pretty darn good idea that back in the States somebody was going to be assigned to make sure the package stayed safe at the local post office till Nannie claimed it. And that immediately thereafter, some other discreet officials would call on her.

I didn't ask. I didn't volunteer anything, except the information that was going to be released to the press about Nannie's accident. The consulate provided a driver to return me to the hotel. That, if anything, showed me how seriously they were taking the whole matter.

C.D. was waiting for me and pacing the lobby floor. "Where have you been?" he demanded as he followed me to my new room.

"I went to the consulate," I said with dignity. "Nannie told me to."

"What for?"

"To get our write-ups and the journal sent back to the States."

"You shouldn't have risked it. You should have taken me with you. Don't you know by now you're a walking target?"

"You think you're not when you're with me?" I blurted out.

We stood there staring at each other. C.D. ran his fingers through his hair. "I can take care of myself, which is more than you can! Anyway, if I want to risk my life, it's my business."

All at once we were in the middle of a terrible fight. Maybe it was inevitable. We'd been through so much together, in so short a time, and we'd grown so close. All those things scared us. Which was why I felt breathless and suffocated, and probably he did, too.

"Are you trying to say if I risk my life it's *not* my business?" I shouted. "What do you mean, I can't take care of myself? Because I'm a woman?"

"Stop putting words in my mouth!" C.D. yelled. "I

don't want to risk your getting hurt!" He said *hurt*; he meant *killed*. He didn't say it, any more than I said I was afraid that could happen to him. The way we felt about each other was suddenly a presence in the room, and we avoided acknowledging the obvious. It was too much to deal with. It was easier to fight.

"Why the hell have you suddenly stopped trusting me?" C.D. demanded.

"I *haven't!* I just don't want you playing guard dog for me." Why couldn't he understand that I needed privacy? And independence—particularly when I was ashamed of how I'd leaned on him, taking advantage of his protectiveness and putting him in danger?

Why did he have to take what I was saying the wrong way? "If all I am to you is a guard dog," C.D. said, his face darkening, "maybe I should just go."

"Maybe you should," I said steadily. "I'll be just fine."

"The hell you will . . . after somebody got into the suite last night—"

"Then you don't think that was just my feminine imagination?"

"Don't put words in my mouth!"

"I'm sorry," I said, and meant it. I sat down abruptly, my legs feeling weak. To my shame, tears came into my eyes. "Honestly, C.D., I really need to be alone. I'll be okay. I'm in a different room. Besides, I'm pretty sure it was the police who were in the suite last night."

C.D. wanted to know why, and I told him because of all Monsieur Guillaume had said. I said go back to his own hotel, please, I'd call if I needed him. I'd see him in the morning. C.D. looked at me for a long minute, said, "On one condition. You keep that gun with you, okay?" kissed me, and left.

I didn't know whether I was relieved or sad.

I did know I'd better get that gun, and so I did. It dawned on me that I wasn't nearly as afraid of guns as I was a week ago, and I didn't know whether to be relieved or sad about that, either. I took a bath, first angling the bathroom door so the full-length mirror on the inside reflected the bedroom entrance. I'd double-locked it, but I wasn't taking chances. I even rested the gun on the tub's rim while I soaked and scrubbed, which was ridiculous.

Afterward, I got dressed and went to the hotel dining room for dinner. No wonder I felt claustrophobic, eating in the suite so much! Nothing out of the ordinary happened during dinner.

I went back to the room and tried to watch an English movie on the VCR. But I couldn't concentrate. Everything kept whirling through my brain. Like a whirling dervish— we'd seen an example of dervish dancing at that "Berber camp" where we'd had the couscous dinner.

Nannie's face when she'd shone the flashlight on Alvarez's body. Nannie and the snake. Nannie lunging forward with the rolled magazine; being struck down. The footsteps in the Marrakech medina. The sound of the amphora breaking. The sight of the worn leather notebook tumbling out. The salt taste of fear. The smell of death—death at the market butcher stalls; death in the garden; death in the street.

And much earlier, back in Texas, Nannie's voice on the telephone, laughing. Nannie saying she'd rescue me from the debutante ball. Saying "There are some things in the Mediterranean I would like to see again." *She hadn't been rescuing me; she'd been using me. As a cover.* Nannie's voice, flat, denying she'd go back to her old career. *I'd meant photography, she'd been thinking O.S.S.*

Nannie writing that letter to me, laboriously, with her left hand. Explaining everything.

Not quite everything, and too late.

Not who the Jaguar was. Not why she'd come back to Morocco *now.*

Some of that I could suddenly guess. She'd had to leave the journal here when she exited Tangier so quickly, and she'd married Granddaddy while she was in England. Granddaddy certainly hadn't wanted to do any overseas travel, and he hadn't wanted Nannie going anywhere without him. He'd been, I realized, passionately in love with her till the day he died. And in all those years she'd never told him he hadn't been her first love, not even her second.

In all those years she'd never tried to retrieve the journal. Why?

Because she'd been told the Jaguar was dead.

Okay. Then why now?

Because she knew he *wasn't* dead? Or was there something special about this moment, now?

To every thing there is a season, and a time—

Like a good little Sunday school girl, I'd brought my Bible with me. Or, rather, Mama had packed it in my suitcase. I got it and turned to the third chapter of Ecclesiastes.

To every thing there is a season, and a time to every pur-
pose under the heaven:
A time to be born, and a time to die; a time to plant,
and a time to pluck . . .
A time to kill, and a time to heal . . . A time to weep,
and a time to laugh; a time to mourn, and a time to
dance . . .
A time to get, and a time to lose . . . a time to keep
silence, and a time to speak . . .

Nannie had decided it was time to break the silence. I'd
seen her do it before, very deliberately, in front of a room
full of people. And then, just as now, all hell had broken
loose. . . .

I saw that scene again: the party at the villa, the
moment when the room went still. Nannie extending her
hand to be kissed; C.D.'s flash going off; Nannie's
attempt to smooth things over; my being pumped for
information about C.D. And then, superimposed on that,
I saw another scene: the moment I'd photographed in
front of the Fatman's gallery—

The pieces of the puzzle suddenly came together in a
blaze of light.

The telephone shrilled.

With nerveless fingers I reached for it, and my voice
rasped. "Yes?"

"Mademoiselle?" It was the hotel manager himself.
"You left instructions not to give out your room number,
but I thought I should relay this message. The night
switchboard operator called me about it personally, since

it sounded urgent. A Mr. Clarence called. He must see you and Madame Clay immediately. He cannot come here. He begs you to come to the establishment of your mutual friend."

"Thank you," I said mechanically, and put down the receiver. I was thinking hard.

Mr. Clarence. That was an alias C.D. might have used—except that he hated the name Clarence so. *Must see me and Madame Clay . . .* He knew Nannie wasn't here.

C.D. hadn't made that call. Unless he was trying to give me some kind of warning.

Our mutual friend's establishment—Max's gallery.

Somebody was setting a trap for me. No, for me and Nannie. Somebody who didn't know Nannie's true situation. And C.D. may have been forced into going along—

All this flashed through my mind in another of those lightning blazes, and at the same instant I knew what I had to do.

I picked up the phone again and called C.D.'s hotel. Waited, heart pounding, while the operator tried to rouse him and then, annoyed at my insistence, went to C.D.'s room, where he picked up the phone to inform me C.D. wasn't there.

I cut the connection; got the hotel manager. Told him where I was going; told him if he didn't hear from me in half an hour he must call the name I provided at the American consulate. Cut him off before he could ask questions, leaving him—I hoped—too alarmed to do anything but follow orders.

Then, working swiftly, I applied kohl eyeliner, coiled up

my hair, put on a caftan and a head scarf. Looking like a native woman, I'd be in less danger on the street. Granddaddy's gun dropped heavily into my pocket.

A trap had been set, and I was going to walk right into it. A lot of people would probably think me crazy. A lot of people would think I didn't have to go, but I knew better. I would risk the danger, as Nannie had risked danger forty-five years before. Because C.D. might be in danger; because Nannie and her secret, which was suddenly my secret, were certainly in danger. Okay, I was a fool to go alone. I could have had the manager get me a police escort. But I couldn't risk that. Nannie had come here on a mission, and now I was on a mission of my own. To bring out the truth—but in the way she wished it done.

I slipped out of the hotel into the street, and like a wraith through the streets. Keeping my eyes down, but with all my other senses burning like raw nerves.

I went by foot, because that seemed safer than risking a possibly phony cab. And I had just turned onto the side street where the gallery was located when suddenly, like that other night, a shadow loomed.

Three shadows. Three men in djellabas, facing me. No one, this time, grabbing me from behind. So they didn't mean to kill me. At least not yet.

Two men stood side by side, slightly concealing the third, who stood behind. Moonlight touched the edge of the first man's profile. Young, very handsome. The man from the photograph, the man from Hassan's shop, the man who had approached me at the party that first night with Nannie. Not one of Mme. Guillaume's protégés. One of General Argenteuil's aides.

I looked straight at him, and he and the other aide shifted weight slightly, and there he was. General Argenteuil himself, the hood of his djellaba thrown back, his hawk-like profile and gleaming hair silvered by the moonlight.

"Bonsoir, Jaguar," I said clearly.

20   The aides' muscles tensed. Argenteuil lifted one hand, then let it fall, and they relaxed and moved apart. Catlike, waiting—I was not fooled by that apparent relaxation. One wrong move, and—

"Miss Clay," General Argenteuil said. "You are an intelligent young woman. You have something that I want."

"No, I don't," I said boldly.

"I said you were intelligent. It would be foolish to deny—"

"I mean," I said, "that I don't have it anymore."

I saw one aide's hand move. The general made another sharp gesture, and then he frowned. "Where is your grandmother?"

"Where you can't find her. The press release was a hoax. She was very badly hurt. She was almost killed. But of course you know that."

"In war or politics, there are many things duty demands that the private man or woman regrets deeply. Nance understood that; I hope she has taught you that truth, too." All at once it was as if Argenteuil and I were alone. He was speaking to me as adult, adversary, equal. As if I were Nannie—now, or forty-five years ago—

All at once we were in a negotiating session. Like politics. Or war.

"Miss Clay—Victoria, if I may . . . please understand

me. You have something that I must have. Give it to me, and take your grandmother back to the States. It would not be difficult. If she is ill, sedated, you can arrange to have her placed on a plane. I can make it possible for you to do so. I do not wish to kill you. Or your grandmother. But I will, if it is necessary."

"I'm quite aware of that," I answered coldly.

"I spared your grandmother's life once before. For love. Now there is more at stake. The future of France."

"You mean your vision of it, don't you? A return to fascism."

"Not fascism! A restoration of France to her former glory. De Gaulle carried her part of the way, but not far enough. And since de Gaulle, there have been"—he shrugged fastidiously—"other influences. Communists. The proletariat."

"Don't you mean the will of the people?"

"Victoria, you are very young. The people do not always know what is best for them. They are not capable of handling great visions and great truths."

Maybe it was that word *truth* that did it. My head came up. "What truth?" I said softly. "The truth that you're willing to let your underlings murder the woman that you loved? That you still love." That drew blood; I knew it. I saw a muscle flicker in his face, and the aides' faces darkened. "General, you are a patriot, a man of honor. A man like that does not take life lightly."

"I have said I will not. If you give me the journal." There, he had put it into words. "I am, as you say, a man of honor."

"I don't have it. It's on its way by diplomatic pouch

153

back to the States. The American embassy does not know what it is; no one does, but me. And Nannie. Nannie doesn't even know I have it. If you let us return home safely, I give you my word of honor I will send it to you."

I was lying as smoothly and automatically as if I had had espionage training. Like him. Like Nannie. There *was* a time for truth, and a time for lies, and if I was wrong about that, may God have mercy on my soul.

For an instant I thought he bought it. But the aides were afraid he had, too. Suddenly there was a gun in the hand of the one on the left, and it was pointed straight at me. In the instant it took him to get it there, I had Granddaddy's pistol in my hand, still in my pocket. My thumb released the safety catch.

I fired a split second before he did, straight through the silver-shot folds of the silken caftan. The aide on the left fell, clutching his right arm. Blood spurted from it, black in the moonlight, and his gun dropped and skittered on the pavement.

"I forgot to tell you," I said sweetly as Argenteuil stared at me. "My granddaddy taught me to be real good with guns."

"So I see," the Jaguar said dryly.

It was, more than ever, a meeting between equals. I was a little more than equal now.

"I don't like using them," I went on conversationally. "But I do when I have to. Just like you do." The other aide made an imperceptible movement, and the barrel of my gun swung toward him. "There are things that matter more than life to me, too. Just like with you—people I love, and the good of France."

"What do you want?" the Jaguar asked quietly.

"I don't want to kill you. I don't even necessarily want to show your journal to the C.I.A. I'm like Nance O'Neill, and you and she are . . . *personnages d'honneur.* We won't use the diary if you will withdraw, immediately and forever, from politics. Retire to your *auberge* in the south of France. . . ."

He was wavering. I knew he was wavering.

In the momentary stillness, the other aide moved. The one who'd followed me. His eyes gleamed with a fanatic's gleam, and his gun came up.

At the same moment, he fired, and the Jaguar made a move, and *I* fired. His shot missed, because the Jaguar had knocked his arm out of the way. My shot did not.

And then, like an anticlimax, came the sound of sirens. Came C.D., on the run. Suddenly the Jaguar was no longer there, only I and two wounded men. Maybe one dead man.

C.D. held out his arms, and I ran into them.

21 It was hours before C.D. and I were alone. All at once, hard on C.D.'s heels, the police were there. An ambulance was there—the two men were hustled into it, in the whirling red lights of the ambulance and police cars, and rushed away. Everything had a strange, psychedelic quality—there was blood, black and thick and gleaming, spattered on my caftan. There was blood on the men's bodies; blood in the street.

Bodies. Was the second man alive or dead? Nobody would tell me anything. I fought against C.D.'s well-meant attempts to soothe me. I shouted at the policemen's insistent attempts, in English, French, and Arabic, to ask me questions. *"I am an American citizen. I won't answer anything until I've spoken with someone from the American consulate."* I kept saying that over and over, to the police, to Monsieur Guillaume when he appeared at the police station where C.D. and I were grilled and fingerprinted.

Finally, at last, two men I'd met at the consulate arrived to guide me through a very guarded statement. They got me free, and they and C.D. returned me to the hotel.

They posted U.S. military guards outside the entrances back at the suite, and C.D. stayed inside with me. We didn't sleep—we sat on the sofa and held each other tightly.

"Don't try to talk. Unless you want to," C.D. said gently.

"I don't know what I want." I stopped. "Yes, I do. I want to know how you got there."

"I got an urgent message at my hotel, telling me to meet you *and* Mrs. Clay at Max's," C.D. said. "I knew it was a setup because the message was supposed to be from you. I was pretty sure they'd call you, too—I mean, why would they want just me? So I rushed over here to try to stop you from going. But I was too late. And by the time I got to Max's street, it was all over."

All at once I started to laugh. "I tried to get you, too. Isn't it ironic?"

C.D. got alarmed. "Tori, don't start that crazy laughing! Want me to take you to your grandmother? I'll get you out of here if you say the word."

"*No!*" I started to shake, and C.D. held me tighter. And sometime or other I fell asleep. I woke in the morning to find us sprawled side by side on the sofa, and I was still held protectively in his arms.

There was one thing C.D. couldn't protect me from. I'd shot two men. I might have killed one. I didn't know. It was the worst thing I could possibly have imagined, but in the morning another horror happened. No one would tell me. *Nobody.*

C.D. at my insistence got a morning paper, but there was nothing in it about any shooting. "Not surprising, is it?" C.D. muttered grimly. There *was* an announcement from General Argenteuil. It was issued from his "new home in Switzerland," and stated tersely that he had retired, effective immediately, from political and public life "for medical reasons."

"Ha," said Nannie when she read this. C.D. and Monsieur Guillaume and I were with her at the hospital, and she looked at me with penetrating eyes. I avoided them, and kept my mouth shut, grateful that Monsieur Guillaume's presence meant we couldn't talk. It wasn't just my taken-for-granted picture of my grandmother that was shattered now. I didn't know myself any better than I'd known her.

There was nothing in any newspaper about the aides whom I had shot.

C.D. took me back to the hotel. Sometime during that endless night I'd told him the truth about my meeting with Argenteuil, but not the whole truth. There were times when that wasn't called for. But *I* needed to know it, and as the day went on, it became apparent I wasn't going to. Not even from that top man from the consulate, whom I suspected but wasn't sure was from the C.I.A. He came to see me that afternoon, and he was very vague.

The United States, France, and Morocco had put their diplomatic heads together, obviously, to keep things hushed up. The only information being released was that an unidentified French fanatic follower of General Argenteuil had been arrested for involvement in three murders—of Hector Alvarez, the Fatman, and the man whom Nannie'd killed.

"Was he one of the men shot?" I asked harshly, and was answered only by a bland smile.

"Miss Clay, I really think you should make an effort to forget about all that. Fortunately, there's no necessity for your name to come up in the matter at all. So, you see, nothing happened."

Except something *had* happened. I'd shot two men, one of whom might be dead.

I was pretty sure the American government—maybe the French and Moroccan governments as well—knew the truth. I did not. All I got, when I got anything at all, was a tangled web of cover-up.

According to the cover story, Alvarez, the Fatman, and the man who'd tried to grab Nannie and me had all been "disposed of" because they'd been involved in blackmailing Argenteuil about some torrid, probably scandalous love affair. That was a story which, if it got out, would only add to the legend of General Argenteuil *(vive la France; vive l'amour).* And it wouldn't hurt the men who were dead.

"The Fatman," Nannie said when she heard of it, "would probably have gotten a kick out of it." It was my next visit to the hospital, when we were at last alone.

She told me about her dealings with the Fatman in the Resistance—and Alvarez, too. When she had finished, I didn't say much, and after a long silence she looked at me directly.

"Tori." Her tone was gentle and very quiet. "I know what happened that night. My contact at the consulate told me. Tori, is there anything you want to say to me?"

"No, ma'am."

"Darling, are you all right? Really?"

"I'm just fine! Even better, now we know you're getting out of here soon."

I thought I heard Nannie sigh. "I'm glad C.D.'s been

looking after you," she said at last. "Just remember, I'm here, too."

"I know that, Nannie." But my voice sounded false, and I got out of there as soon as I could.

C.D. and I went swimming that afternoon, and then we went out dancing. We stayed out very late, and we danced up a storm. And then we went back to the hotel, still laughing, still feeling giddy, and I found a box waiting for me in the suite, placed there by the manager of the hotel.

Inside was Granddaddy's gun, returned to me by the Tangier police. I took one look at it, and my control shattered like exploding glass.

I started to cry, and then I started to moan. I moaned and moaned, hugging my stomach, bent double as though from a mortal wound. C.D. caught me and eased me to the floor. We knelt there, and I clung to him like a lifeline.

"*Say it*," C.D. said strongly.

"I don't know what you mean!" I shook my head blindly. "Get rid of that thing! I don't ever want to see it again!"

"No," C.D. said. He picked the gun up and held it between us, its metal darkly gleaming. So small, so lethal. "Look at it, Tori. Look at it. Don't look away. You used it, and you have to come to terms with that."

"You think I don't know it?" I shouted in anger now. "I may have killed somebody! I don't even know! No one will tell me! I'm supposed to be a good little girl and forget all about it! *How?*"

"I can't tell you that," C.D. said very quietly.

"There's nobody who can."

"Oh, yes, there is," C.D. answered. And kissed me, and went away.

He meant Nannie, of course. Nannie, who loved me. Nannie, who had killed and gone on living, keeping secrets. But I couldn't talk to her, not until I'd come to terms with what she'd done, and forgiven her. Which in a weird way was more painful, harder, than trying to forgive myself.

22 So the days of hot summer went on, following a circumscribed circle. Morning swim, visit to Nannie in the hospital, back to the hotel and some desultory shopping or sightseeing ... lunch in a street café or by the pool, usually with C.D. ... a siesta in the suite or under an umbrella on the pool terrace, my nose usually in a book in an unsuccessful effort to blot out thought ... then back to the hospital, and more sightseeing, and eventually dinner. And dancing. Almost always dancing. The only time I *really* didn't think was when I was in C.D.'s arms, drowning in the beat of pulsing music.

Either I slept a lot, or couldn't sleep at all. C.D. was staying at the suite full-time now, using Nannie's bedroom, and often in the hours before dawn he'd hear me pacing in the sitting room, and come up behind me to wrap his arms around me. It was the only thing that helped. But not enough.

Mail came from my parents, and I answered it. Evasively; lightheartedly. Nannie wrote them, too. "The last thing we need," she said, "much as I love him, is your father flying over here."

"Or Mama," I said. We grinned at each other, and it was almost like things used to be.

Almost.

When Nannie and I talked, which wasn't much, it was

all surface. And that was a change, a terrible change, but one I clung to. Sometimes I thought I couldn't bear the idea of losing forever the grandmother I used to know. But I had lost her. Just as the Tori I used to be was gone forever. Nannie'd lost a starry-eyed hero worshipper, and there was a sadness in her eyes, too, when she looked at me. I knew she ached for me, ached with wishing she could somehow "kiss the hurt and make it go away," and I couldn't bear it.

As the days went on, I could feel myself becoming more and more what I'd judged my mother for: one of the surface people, not allowing myself to feel too deeply or to share.

"Sleeping Beauty," C.D. said once, pointedly, when I'd gone off into one of my silences.

I looked at him blankly.

"You know what I mean," he said back. "I always did think there was a heck of a lot of psychology packed under those old tales."

He never said anything more, directly or indirectly, about my talking to Nannie. And I never heard anything more about the Argenteuil affair—from the police or from the consulate. In fact, the consulate stopped returning my calls.

And, finally, Nannie came home.

She came back to the hotel in state, in an ambulance and with a wheelchair, in early afternoon. A nurse came with her to help settle her in. The hotel management bowed and scraped, and the suite was full of flowers. At last all the outsiders cleared out, and it was just Nannie and C.D. and me.

Almost immediately, C.D. headed for Nannie's room. When he reappeared a minute later, I almost gasped. His camera was slung around his neck, and his camera bag and soft suitcase hung from his shoulder.

"What are you *doing?*" I demanded shrilly.

"Going back to my own place," C.D. said calmly. "You don't need me here anymore, and, anyway, you guys deserve a chance to be alone."

"C.D., don't go!" I said, still in that tinny voice. "You can still stay—there's loads of room here, isn't there, Nan?"

C.D. gave me a long, thoughtful look. "I don't think so," he said. He went over to my grandmother and, to my astonishment, lifted her hand and kissed it. "I'm glad you're back, Mrs. Clay."

"Me, too," Nannie said. Another, similar look passed between them. Then Nannie straightened briskly in her wheelchair. "You'll come back for dinner with us this evening, hear?"

"I don't think—"

"I *do*," Nannie said firmly. C.D. grinned, and saluted, and took his leave.

Nannie and I were alone together.

I turned away, and then, involuntarily, I glanced back. She didn't see me; she was gazing toward the French doors to our private garden. And for the first time in weeks, the first time since the night Alvarez died, I really saw her. All that energy, all that *presence* seemed to have gone with C.D.'s leaving, as if it had been a mask she'd worn. She looked weary. She looked *old*. She looked as though she'd shrunken into herself on the shiny chair.

Suddenly I was speaking around an aching lump that filled my throat.

"Nan . . . why don't you go to bed? You look beat."

"I think I will," Nannie said tiredly. "Jouncing over uneven streets in an ambulance is not my idea of a good time."

She wheeled herself, insistently independent, into her bedroom, and I helped her transfer with difficulty from chair to bed. She was wearing a caftan, so there was nothing tight she had to struggle out of. I covered her with the embroidered sheer cotton spread and left her in the shuttered dimness.

When I looked in a short while later, she was asleep. I lay down in my own room, but sleep would not come. After a while I jumped up, put on my bathing suit, and went to the outdoor pool. The sun was hot at this hour, and there weren't many people there, except some flight attendants and pilots killing time between trips. I stayed at the other end of the pool terrace, huddled beneath an umbrella, and after a while I dove into the pool and started swimming laps, driving myself until my eyes stung and my lungs were aching. When I finally went back to the suite, Nannie was up, and dressing with the assistance of a hotel maid. She was splendid in a green-and-silver caftan, so I dressed up to match.

C.D., when he arrived, also looked as if he'd made a special effort. We were all making an effort at normalcy, as if we were ordinary tourists, as if the events of the past weeks had never been. We sat in the hotel lounge, drinking iced fruit juice from tall crystal glasses in silver holders, and then we went to the dining room and feasted on crown roast of lamb, tiny Mediterranean vegetables, and tropical fruits, winding up with Arabic coffee in the lounge.

And we made bright, clever chitchat. My mother would have been proud of me. I wasn't.

When the brass coffeepot was empty, C.D. looked at us. "You guys going to call it a night, or go listen to the music in the ballroom? It sounds pretty good."

"You young people stay and dance. I'm going to turn in, if you'll be kind enough to push me to the suite, C.D.," Nannie said. "No, Tori, you stay. I've already arranged for the maid to come in and help me. C.D. will be back with you in minutes."

So I stayed, as I'd been told to, and I wondered what was going on between my grandmother and C.D. during that journey through the hotel corridors. Not much, apparently; C.D. was back almost at once. And we danced and danced, until my legs ached from dancing and my face from smiling. Long after midnight, C.D. walked me to the suite. He left me at the door after kissing me briefly, gently, and I had again that sense that things were changing.

I let myself into the dim and silent suite. Nannie was asleep; I could hear the sound of her soft breathing. I undressed in the dark, and crept into bed, and fell almost at once into a dreamless sleep.

What awakened me I don't know; one minute I was unconscious and the next I was bolt upright, wide awake. And shivering. The suite wasn't cold, but I was shivering. I hugged myself, feeling my ribs beneath my shaking fingers. I'd lost weight. After a while I jumped out of bed and threw a robe around my shoulders, and went out into the sitting room. I could not stay still; I kept pacing up and down.

I was afraid, and that was crazy. The nightmare was over, there was no more danger. But I was gripped by terror, a terror deeper and more intense than that I'd felt those terrible nights in the Tangier streets. And a grief that was like a lead weight in my chest and bent me double.

Suddenly, my eyes were burning. But they were dry. A dry sob wrenched me.

"Don't fight it," a quiet voice said behind me.

Nannie. Nannie, in the wheelchair into which she had, with God knew how much effort, dragged herself. I stared at her and she said again, "Let the tears come, Tori."

"I *can't.*"

"Yes, you can. You must. There's no need to keep up a facade."

"Who are you to talk about facades—" The words were torn from me. I gasped, a gasp that was like a cry, and clasped a hand across my shaking mouth.

"Stop it," Nannie said sternly, quietly. And then, "Oh, my darling heart, don't you know there's no need with me?"

It was so much a bitter twist of scenes from childhood that involuntarily I laughed.

"That's better," Nannie said, watching me. "Laughter and tears are two sides of the same coin. Two Janus faces." She looked off toward the garden, where a little Arabic slipper of a moon was shining, and her face was sad and tender. "Remember how your granddaddy used to tell you all the old Greek and Roman legends? Remember Janus, the god of doorways? With two different faces, one looking outward, one in. One backward, and one forward. I remember him telling you that's why the first month of the year takes its name from Janus."

I nodded. "I remember you reading me fairy tales," I said thickly, and suddenly the memory of C.D.'s comment about Sleeping Beauty rose.

Nannie nodded. "You always hated some of them," she said as if she'd read my mind. "The dark fairy tales, that had two levels. You couldn't bear the shadow side. Which always puzzled me, considering how uncompromising you always were about the truth. What's hurting you the most, Tori? The fact that there was a shadow side of Nance O'Neill, or the fact that you didn't know it?"

The suddenness and unerringness of the question made me gasp again.

"I don't know," I said at last. "I don't know what's bothering me. I know part of it's discovering that there's a shadow side to *me*."

Nannie nodded. "Didn't you tell me you read Arthur Miller's *The Crucible* in school last year? You remember what John Proctor's wife says to him? That it doesn't matter who else forgives you, if you won't forgive yourself?"

"*How?*" I demanded. "How in God's name did you ever do it? I may have killed somebody, Nan! How can I live with that? How do *you?*"

"I do, because I have to." Nannie gave me a level look that caught and held me. "Tell yourself the truth, Victoria. If you had to live that night with the Jaguar over again, would you have done anything differently?"

It was my gaze that fell.

"You did what you had to do," Nannie said, more gently. "Because you have honor, and integrity, and you could not allow the killing to continue—allow the Jaguar to go on—any more than I could. When I recognized his photo in the paper a few months ago, and saw that *he* was the famous General Argenteuil, I knew I had to come back for that journal, to finally get it to the authorities. I couldn't *not* come, any more than I could have allowed you to be killed that other night. We acted out of instinct, out of conscience."

She paused and looked at me; I was silent. Then she went on. "Because the adult truth behind the fairy tales, my darling, is that we don't live in a world of blacks and whites, but of many colors—sometimes of shades of gray. And sometimes we have to choose, not between good and evil, but between what will do the most good, or the least harm. For the most people. Over the long haul."

"I hate it," I said passionately.

"But there's not one thing you can do about it," Nannie said. "And that's the truth."

Tears started in my eyes, and my heart was pounding. But, oddly, my body didn't hurt as much anymore. I wasn't stiff and shaking.

"I can't even find out if I killed that guy, Nan," I said huskily. "No one will tell me."

"You may never know. You'll just have to live with that." Nannie's face softened. "Welcome to adulthood, darling."

The tears started running, and I didn't hold them back. My grandmother held out her arms, and I stumbled into them.

Later, much later, as dawn was coming up outside our windows, I asked Nan shyly, "That—magazine trick. You'd used it before, hadn't you? During the war?"

Nannie looked at me calmly. "Do you really want to know?"

I shook my head.

I didn't ask what she intended doing with the Jaguar's journal, either. That was her business. She could tell me when and if she wanted to. By which time, I thought humbly, maybe I'll understand things better.

There were times and seasons for everything, even seemingly wrong things like loss and death. Maybe never knowing the *whole* truth—or understanding it—was part of being human. "For now we see through a glass darkly," as St. Paul wrote.

I knew this much. I'd mellowed since I'd left home. Maybe it was all the terror, and maybe it was love. Maybe I'd just grown up. At least I no longer confused diplomacy with being two-faced. And I'd come to the conclusion that just maybe, there was sometimes something more important than being truthful—doing what was *right*.

Things I'd done, things Nannie'd done, wouldn't be right in a perfect world. But we weren't in a perfect world, and we'd had to choose, as Nannie'd said, not between black and white, but between shades of gray. And I knew, looking back, that if I had to do it all again, I'd still do as I had done. I only hoped God understood.

23 I guess I don't have to say my mother and father weren't told the total story. "We'd better leave them in blessed innocence," Nannie said. Though what story she intends to tell them if or when she gets her rumored Legion of Honor, I'm afraid to think.

Oh, yes—that party at the American embassy in Rabat, in honor of General Argenteuil. It was, needless to say, called off. But Nannie and I did go to a party there, and C.D., too. That was much later, a whole two months later. Two months Nannie and I spent in Morocco while she recovered, and C.D. spent bopping around the map of Europe, with frequent return visits to Rabat, where Nannie and I were staying.

C.D. and I were growing closer all the time, which was not surprising, considering what we'd been through together. We both knew it, but didn't speak of it—there was no need. Nannie knew it, too, but kept her mouth shut, figuring, I guess, that it was up to me to handle the fireworks at home after I returned.

Meanwhile, at the end of summer, we went to a gala at the American embassy at which Nance O'Neill was the honored guest. Nannie was very elegant, on crutches but in a splendid caftan, purple silk embroidered and shot with gold. I wore a caftan, too, as did many other guests, and C.D. was splendid in a rented tux.

The gala was, as Nannie said, modern luxury masquerading as old Morocco. I just laughed. I didn't mind masquerades so much anymore. Dinner was served in a tent considerably more splendid than the one on the trip from Marrakech. The grounds were covered with velvety rugs, and we sat on silken cushions and ate from brass trays with our fingers—three fingers of the right hand only. There was dancing, there was singing, there was music on pipes and on stringed instruments. And just before sunset, cymbals announced the commencement of a fantasia.

I don't know how to describe it except that it was like a medieval joust on Arabian horses. The riders were dressed as Moors in the service of a medieval potentate. Banners waved in the breeze, and the horses wheeled and dashed, and silver lances glinted in the setting sun.

I watched, and my eyes filled with tears. It was so beautiful—and something more. C.D.'s arm tightened around me, and he bent to kiss me. I knew he, too, felt the magic. We'd stepped into another culture, another time, together—as we'd stepped into a world of danger, a reincarnation of the days of World War II, together. And we'd found depths in each other we'd never have found any other way.

What was that phrase I'd used to the Jaguar? *Personnage d'honneur*. A person of honor. C.D. was one. And so was Nannie. That was all the truth I needed now.

In two more days, we'd all be going home. Nannie to her plantation and being Mrs. Henry McCausland Clay. Me to my senior year of high school. C.D. back to college. Some way, somehow, somewhere he and I would be together. There *would* be a time for love.